PINK F*CKING MOSCATO

ANNA REZES

WORDS
IMAGINED

To everyone who failed so hard but found the courage to get back up.

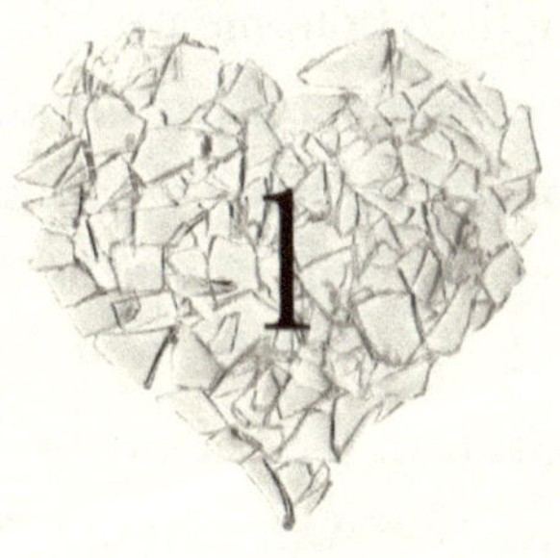

WILLA

The envelope was heavy—expensive. I held it in my hands, turning it over. The shiny cream paper weighed me down. I recognized the names on the return label—Evan and Estelle. It used to be Evan and Willa and to associate his name with another woman felt cruel. My chest constricted like my torso was caught in the vise grip of a giant, but it wasn't a giant that held me. It was fear—fear that Evan still had the power to hurt me.

I wanted to pretend I wasn't so weak. I knew this day was coming, but even still, the envelope sat in my hand like a bomb waiting to go off.

Throw it away. I told myself. But I had to see it. I had to confirm this was real so I could move on with my life.

It was just a piece of paper. It had no power over me. I pulled the card out of the envelope, and for a moment, I was confused. Then, as if realizing I was holding a poisonous snake, I threw the card and tried to scream, but choked instead as my throat narrowed, imprisoning my cry for help.

I turned, gripping the kitchen chair while a sob caught in

my throat. I whimpered as my body shook. My legs no longer possessed the strength to hold me upright, and my knees met the tile floor as violent sobs rocked through me, ripping and tearing their way out of me. I clung to the chair as if it could save me from this agony while my tears dotted the floor like drops of rain.

My mother walked in the back door. When she saw me, she dropped the bags she was carrying. She asked me what was wrong as she knelt beside me. I wanted to say *everything,* but when I opened my mouth to speak, a horrible wail tore its way out of me. I released the chair that had failed me and instead clung to my mother—my savior.

Paper may not have the power to hurt me, but the words written on that paper knocked the air from my lungs and shattered a piece of my soul. I couldn't go through this. Not again. I had to get away. I needed a timeout, just long enough to catch my breath.

*I*t's completely irrational—this attraction I have to men wearing backpacks. I can't explain it. There is something masculine and sexy about a grown man wearing a bag strapped across his muscular back. This man especially. His hand stroked the dark stubble of his cheek down his jaw while his feet shifted.

Maybe it was just my sleep deprivation that made me think his backpack made him more attractive. I barely slept the night before. I was ready to leave right after I opened the mail from my ex, but my mom convinced me to wait until the next morning. So, while I spent the night in the twin bed of my childhood bedroom, Evan was probably wrapped around a naked Estelle in their adult-sized bed.

With little sleep, I got up early and spent most of my day driving. The goal was to go further north, but I had to stop because my eyes were too heavy. I pulled off at a rest area and looked up hotels on my phone, finding one with glowing reviews just off the next exit. I booked a room, and now, here I was.

The hotel looked newly renovated, but something was wrong with the lobby doors. They continued to slide open and closed despite no one being around to activate them. Warm Michigan air swept through the lobby, blowing my long hair into my face. I gathered up the dark strands, twisting them into a quick braid. I had nothing to secure the ends, so I left them loose.

The lobby wasn't crowded, but the guests standing at the counter were an utter pain in the ass. As the couple bickered over rooms, the clerk assisting them tried to excuse himself, but the couple reeled him back in with more questions, like what side of the building did the rooms face, is there a Jacuzzi in the room, could they get a free upgrade, and could the hotel guarantee the surrounding rooms had quiet occupants. The clerk's responses kept getting shorter and more direct, but the couple was undeterred.

Meanwhile, the line grew behind them. Well, sort of. It was only the sexy backpack man with his bottle of Pink Moscato and me. Curious. He held the incredibly feminine bottle of wine with confidence, masculine confidence that said, I'm not drinking this alone. And by the looks of him, I had no doubt he had someone waiting for him upstairs. She was probably gorgeous and sprawled across his bed wearing a lacy teddy and eating chocolate-covered strawberries. Except no one was that romantic anymore—unless she was his mistress. I looked for a wedding ring and didn't find one. Figures, he would've taken it off for his midweek fling.

I wasn't always so cynical, but after seeing my husband of six years in bed with another woman, my heart and mind were pretty fucking disillusioned with love. Now I saw affairs everywhere I looked. Thank you, Evan Durban, my son-of-a-bitch ex.

Another hotel attendant came out from the back and walked to the second computer. She smiled pleasantly at the man in front of me, and he took a step forward. He asked her for a corkscrew, saying he forgot his. As she went to the back to grab one, he leaned against the counter, his fingers tapping quietly against the granite while he waited. He looked to be in his late twenties, same as me. His hair was long enough for a man bun, and it irritated me because it looked so good on him. He wore a pastel blue t-shirt with light pink shorts and somehow; he pulled that off too. He had a carefree air about him, and his feet were in sandals like some kind of bohemian love child. I was staring a hole in the back of his head when the obnoxious couple stepped away from the counter.

I moved forward and gave the clerk my name so he could look up the reservation I'd just made. I booked it under Willa Durban because that's the name on my credit cards, but I was looking to change all of that. I wasn't psyched to go back to my maiden name, Willa Rose. It might sound cute, but I was so tired of the comments. I just wanted a regular name, which I had until Evan took it away. Bastard.

The clerk found my reservation, and because I couldn't help it, I asked, "My room isn't close to the couple that just left is it?"

Backpack guy tried to smother his laughter by coughing. I glanced at him, and his eyes snagged on mine, his lips turning up into a slight grin. Oh, hell. His look sent a zing of electricity through me. No matter how much humans evolved, sexual desire was an instinct. And no matter how hard we fought our biology, our libido always fought back.

And the bitch never fought fair. We may act like superior beings, but deep down, I knew we were all just animals playing pretend.

I turned my attention back to the clerk, seeing he was also wearing a smile, though not nearly as sexy. "No, ma'am, you are on a different floor."

"Thank you," I said gratefully, while the woman returned with a corkscrew in hand.

"Sorry," she said to the bohemian love child. "It wasn't where it was supposed to be. It's the only one we have so you'll have to use it here."

"No problem," he said as he opened his Pink Moscato. He gave the device back with a very polite thank you before heading toward the elevators.

The clerk handed me my room card, pointing me in the same direction as Mr. Pink Moscato. I walked my scrubby ass over to wait for the elevator. After spending all day driving, I wanted to shower and go to bed. My nerves pricked as I stood next to the attractive stranger.

The elevator dinged open, and Mr. Polite held out his arm, gesturing for me to go first. I stepped in, rolling my eyes at his gentlemanly behavior. I went to stand in the corner, and he followed. He stood by the panel of buttons, and I realized I hadn't pushed the one for my floor.

"What floor?" he asked, looking back at me with his light blue eyes.

"Three, please," I said in a small voice.

He nodded, saying, "Me too." He pressed the little three, and the doors slid shut, locking us in together.

As the elevator rose, he leaned back, crossing one

sandaled foot over the other. On our ride up, he asked, "Are you traveling for business?"

The question felt invasive, not to mention dumb. My cut-off shorts and spaghetti strap top weren't professional. When I looked up at him, I realized he was smiling. He was fucking with me. He made a joke, and I was too stupid to get it. Also, I felt a little insulted.

As the doors opened, I said, "At least I don't look like an Easter egg threw up on me."

He laughed while I climbed off the elevator. I hurried forward liking the sound of his laugh way too much. I wheeled my bag down the hall in search of room three-twelve. Stopping in front of my door, I pulled out the card. Before scanning it, he walked to the other side of me to room three-fourteen.

"Oh, look, we're neighbors."

"Shit," I whispered under my breath. Now I'd have to crank the TV to avoid listening to sex noises all night.

"Something wrong?" he asked.

I flicked my eyes to him as I scanned my key and twisted the handle. "No. Goodnight."

He was opening his door, but he turned to face me with a smirk. "Goodnight? It's four o'clock in the afternoon."

My eyes searched his face while I pivoted my bag. He had a breathtaking smile, and his eyes were alight with humor. But I was so tired of being the butt of the joke, and if he was flirting, I wasn't interested. I turned away, shoving my bag the rest of the way into my room, letting the door slam behind me. I flipped the locks for good measure.

♥ ♥ ♥

IT TOOK ME A FEW MINUTES TO REGISTER THE POUNDING at my door because I was wearing earplugs, plus the TV was blaring. I pulled out my earplugs and heard the noise again, louder this time. I threw my blankets off and grabbed the remote to turn down the TV while I pulled on pants. Looking through the peephole, I saw my new neighbor. He was no longer wearing his Easter outfit, and his carefree bohemian lovechild air had disappeared.

I kept the chain locked as I cracked open the door, not caring if I looked paranoid. I would rather be paranoid than end up raped or dead.

"Yes," I said, peeking through the crack.

He folded his arms over his chest and tilted his head to the side, giving me a dirty look. "Were you asleep?" he asked incredulously.

"I was," I returned irritated.

"For fuck sakes, it's two in the morning! Turn down your TV," he said, running a hand through his hair, before adding, "Please."

Maybe I should feel bad, but instead, I laughed at his attempt at manners. "Since you asked so nicely, I'll turn it down."

He smiled at me, causing me to grip the inside door handle tighter. His smile did things to me. It had been six months since Evan broke my heart and it had been even longer since we'd had sex. And that smile radiated sex. I reeled in my thoughts, realizing I was biting my lip and remembered why I had the TV up so loud in the first place.

I stood up taller. "I didn't mean to disturb you guys. . ." *of your sexcapade.* I didn't say that part out loud.

"Thank you," he said, looking thoughtful. He took a step

toward his door and stopped. He spun back toward me, tilting his head in question. "Us guys?"

"Yeah, you and your girlfriend or whatever."

He stared at me, almost squinting before his face relaxed. A sexy smile curled those lips, bringing dirty thoughts to my head.

He broke those thoughts by saying, "What makes you think I have a girl with me?"

"Umm, the Pink Moscato."

"What if I told you the wine was for me?"

"I'd call you a liar."

"The Pink Moscato is all mine. I'm the only one drinking it," he said.

I rolled my eyes. "Right, okay. Goodnight."

I started to close my door, but he stopped it, pushing back, holding it open as far as the chain would allow. "You didn't call me a liar," he said, his baby blues zeroing in on me.

"It's none of my business. Goodnight," I said again, hoping he would let me close the door.

His eyes continued to appraise me for a moment before he relented. "Goodnight." He removed his arm, and I closed the door.

I flipped the deadbolt and walked back to my bed. I crawled under the fluffy comforter before turning off the TV. As I stared at the blank screen, the lack of sound sunk in, crumbling my composure as everything I lost screamed loudly into the silence. It felt all-consuming.

Trying to hide from it, I pulled the blankets up over my head, curled into a ball, and began singing the song my mother sang to me when I was young. My voice was a whisper, barely audible to my own ears. My tears came next, helping me to fill in that empty void that sat inside my chest.

♥ ♥ ♥

WATER HAD ALWAYS SOOTHED ME AND LUCKY FOR ME, the hotel had two pools, one indoor and one outdoor. It was a beautiful day outside with the sun shining while a slight breeze made the eighty-degree weather feel bearable. It was a day everyone wanted to spend outdoors, except for me. While the outdoor pool was crawling with people, the indoor pool was nearly vacant. Setting my things down on an empty chair beside the vacant pool, I removed the sheer white tunic that covered my swimsuit, revealing the black bikini underneath. I'm comfortable enough with my body, and when I tried on the bikini in the dressing room at the store, I felt confident, unstoppable. But standing here now, I realized that I was not invincible, and I have never been comfortable strutting around in a bathing suit of any kind.

So, I did what I do best. I pretended to be confident. I pretended that I was the hottest woman in the room and that I was in total control over my life. I pretended to be here in this hotel because I wanted to be and not because I didn't know how to be anywhere else.

I slipped out of my flip-flops and took a few steps to the edge of the pool. I dipped my toe in and found the water warmer than I had expected. Holding my head high, I walked to the steps at the shallow end. My hand landed on the cool steel rail that ran down the wide concrete steps. As my foot sunk into the water, I imagined I was a model sashaying seductively into the pool. I was ridiculous, but it made me feel sexy, something I hadn't felt in a long time.

When I was waist deep, I dove under, swimming down the length of the pool. It felt refreshing to be under the water. Somehow the quiet down here didn't fill me with all the disparaging thoughts it had last night. This silence felt tranquil. It soothed me in a way nothing else had since, well . . . a long time ago. Years. I was happy once, wasn't I? It felt like a lifetime ago.

My hand reached out to touch the wall of the pool, and my head popped out of the water. My hair suctioned to me, my face caught in a web of long dark strands. I lowered my head under and came up again to free myself of the stray strands. That's when I noticed him. The man from yesterday sat in a chair watching me. I couldn't tell if he had been watching me or if he just happened to look over at that exact moment. He sat close to the seat where I had set my things. We held eye contact for a moment before I noticed the gorgeous woman in the red-string bikini who was approaching him.

He looked over at her with a smile as she sat next to him. She handed him a drink, and the two began talking. *Sure, the Pink Moscato was for him.* Liar.

All men were liars. I already knew this, but I was still disappointed.

I turned and dove back under, pissed that he stole the comfort I was feeling a moment ago. I didn't know why I was letting him get to me. Maybe it's because it had been a long time since anyone had looked at me the way he kept looking at me. It had been even longer since I felt that flutter of excitement he provoked inside of me.

I swam several laps only coming up long enough to breathe. Exercise was good because it released endorphins. Endorphins triggered positive feelings. At least that's what science tells us. I needed all the positive feelings I could get. Maybe I would stay here, swimming laps until my muscles gave out and I drowned. At least I would have positive feelings while I died. Or perhaps science was bullshit. It certainly had let me down in the past.

I didn't swim myself to death, but my muscles were sore and shaking slightly by the time I finished swimming laps. My neighbor was no longer sitting in his chair. In fact, the room had pretty much cleared out. Still, I tried not to be obvious as I searched for him. I hated my attraction to him, and I didn't want to be taken off guard again. Once I decided he was no longer around, I relaxed into the water, closing my eyes and floating on my back before staring up at the giant skylights above the pool. My arms floated out to my sides, and for a moment, everything felt perfect.

Through the windows, I watched the fluffy white clouds pass by, morphing their size and shape as they went. I had to marvel that those clouds may have once been droplets of water in this very pool. It fascinated me how water could change so completely. It was continually transforming—one minute we were swimming in it, the next it was airborne, becoming moisture in the air. It would rise into the atmosphere with all its little water buddies, and together they became frozen crystals that formed fluffy shapes in the sky. And when they were tired of flying, they would fall, splashing down in raging torrents of rain, or floating with the grace of a beautiful snowflake. And every time water fell, it would land somewhere it had never been before, over and over until that drop of water had seen the entire world. I shook my head, snapping out of my thoughts as my body collided with someone.

I pulled up straight, my feet finding the floor of the pool. "Sorry," I said as I turned to see who it was. The rest of my words caught in my throat as Mr. Moscato stood before me bare-chested, looking fucking hot with his sexy wet hair and muscled chest. My nipples stood at attention, and I was thankful the water granted me a little camouflage.

He said nothing at first, so I looked around. There was no one else in the pool or the entire room. I turned back to him, feeling more uneasy now that I knew we were alone. And why was he standing so close to me? I backed up.

He noted my movement and moved the opposite direction, asking, "What were you just thinking about?"

"I was thinking this creepy guy is way too close to me. Where's your girlfriend?"

He shook his head. "I told you, the wine was for me. I don't have a girlfriend."

I gawked at him. "I saw her with you earlier." I turned to the ladder behind me to climb out of the water. "Men are pigs," I said under my breath as I walked to my things.

I threw on my bathing suit cover and towel-dried my hair while I slipped into my flip-flops. A family came in, the kids screaming with excitement.

Suddenly I felt his body behind me. He leaned in, his chest against my back, his proximity drawing the air from the room. His arm came around me to point at the window to the outdoor pool. I looked where he directed and saw the girl in the red bikini sitting in a guy's lap. I closed my eyes as his breath landed against my neck. "If she was my girl, do you think I'd be okay with that? She handed me a beer and asked if I wanted to see her room. I turned her down, and she found someone else. We aren't all pigs."

After his last word, he moved away. When I turned around, he was grabbing his shirt off a chair. Without looking back, he strode out, letting the door slam behind him.

I was breathing heavily, wondering what the hell was going on. "I need a drink."

I was afraid to go back up to my room because I was a chicken. I was worried I'd run into him, and I really didn't want to run into him, but I would not sit in the bar soaking wet. I decided to woman up and go back to my room. I made it there without seeing him.

I took a quick shower, putting more effort into my appearance, hoping it would restore some of my confidence. I already felt pathetic, and going out alone, I would need all the self-assurance I could get.

Evan had stolen the confidence I once had. I used to think I was beautiful. I wasn't full of myself, but I could make myself look good. Now, the long lashes that I thought I had didn't impress me. My brown eyes that used to shine now felt dull. The caramel skin that I used to think of as exotic and unique made me feel different and unusual. My hair, the thing I used to love the most about myself, no longer excited me. My long dark waves used to be full, but the stress of life had thinned that hair that I adored so much. I wasn't going bald, but I didn't feel the same pride I used to feel.

My black sundress was cute. The dress covered the parts of me I didn't like, and the back dipped, showing off the tattoo under my right shoulder blade. I would never have a thigh gap. I was okay with that, but at twenty-nine, my body had been through a lot. I was thankful for my health. I was grateful for everything I had, but I still felt broken. I felt robbed, but I didn't want to stay bitter for the rest of my life.

I tore myself away from the mirror, grabbed my purse and the room key, and before I talked myself out of it, I left. I should have looked before stepping out because as soon as I did, I almost ran into the guy next door.

"Whoa," he said, stepping out of my path while his arm reached out to keep me from plowing into him.

I stopped abruptly, but it didn't prevent my hands from extending themselves. It was a reflex, part of the momentum that was carrying me forward. My hands collided with his chest while his hands grabbed my upper arms and dammit if I didn't feel his touch everywhere.

His hair was pulled back into that damn man bun again and even that was sexy. He grinned at me. "You in a hurry?" He stepped back, releasing me while I did the same.

He asked me a question, but all I could think about was the way his eyes ran down my body and then right back up. It was barely noticeable, but I was staring at him—hard. I shook my head to break the trance. The movement wasn't subtle, and his little snicker told me he saw it.

I cleared my throat, saying, "I'm going down to the bar."

"Oh. The nachos are good."

Oh yeah, I probably should eat. I hadn't thought about food. I just needed alcohol. "I'll keep that in mind," I said.

He stepped toward his door, dismissing me, and I started walking toward the elevators when I heard him call out, "I have more Pink Moscato in my room if you want some."

I hesitated and looked back over my shoulder at him. He shrugged like it was no big deal, but it felt like a proposition to me, and I wasn't amused. "I'll pass," I said, continuing forward.

♥ ♥ ♥

I DIDN'T GET THE NACHOS, BUT I DID GET SOME FOOD TO go with my giant margarita. I had a few guys offer to buy me drinks which was great for my self-esteem despite knowing men were disgusting pigs. My best friend would yell at me for turning down free drinks, but I never felt right accepting them. I felt like free drinks came with unspoken expectations. I also felt guilty that the unwanted attention flattered me. My inner-feminist was disappointed in me.

Once I finished my giant margarita and chicken fingers, I headed back to my room. It was just before seven o'clock and the lobby was packed. From the commotion, I gathered there was a baseball tournament, and the teams were checking in, leaving hordes of teenage boys to meander the lobby.

I just hit the button for the elevator when the doors swung open. Mr. Pink Moscato stepped out, holding a bottle in each hand. He didn't notice me right away. He took a few steps, either deep in thought or just incredibly focused on getting the corkscrew.

"Two bottles this time?" I questioned.

His head snapped up to look at me. Why did I crave his attention so much, but then act like a complete bitch when he talked to me?

I think he tried to smile at me, but it fell short. He nodded his answer, and then we continued to stand there in silence. When I didn't say anything else, he started walking away.

"Wait," I called.

He turned back.

Why was I doing this? Why?

"The lobby is packed," I warned. "It'll take you forever to get through the line. I have a corkscrew upstairs."

When he continued to stand there, I clarified, "You can use it instead of spending half your night in line."

He inhaled deeply and let out a long breath before stepping back toward the elevator. I had to hit the button again, and the doors slid open. We entered leaning against opposite walls to face one another, but he was staring at the floor. Before the doors closed, I asked, "Are you okay?"

He glanced at me with a look so intense; it intimidated me. He shook his head ever so slightly while he said, "I don't know."

"What's wrong?" I normally would not ask such an invasive question to a near stranger, but I couldn't help it.

He folded his arms over his chest, still holding a bottle in each hand. "I don't even like Pink Moscato."

A laugh burst from me. I couldn't help it. It was so unexpected, and I was slightly drunk. "What?"

My laugh seemed to snap him out of his funk because he started laughing too.

"Why are you drinking it?" I asked.

"What else am I going to do with it?"

"Stop buying it!"

The elevator doors opened, and we walked down the hall. I entered my room without worrying about him attacking me. He stood in the doorway while I went to my suitcase.

It took me looking in a few different places before I

found the corkscrew and held it up. "Voila!" I exclaimed, feeling tipsy.

He looked to me and smiled, saying, "My hero!"

As I walked to him, I saw him glance at the dresser piled with all the makeup I pulled out earlier. I hadn't cleaned it up because I had my mini freak-out.

"I'm not usually so messy. I was in a hurry." I looked at him, wondering why I just explained that to him. "I don't know why I told you that."

He shook his head. "You don't need all that."

I laughed. "That's such a guy thing to say. You only say that to make me feel pretty, but the second I stopped wearing it, you'd be like, okay, maybe you are better with it."

"I've never thought that about anyone else. Addison is prettier when she wears makeup. Not saying she's ugly without it, but it enhances what she has. You naturally have dark lashes and beautiful skin."

I felt the heat in my cheeks but pretended it wasn't there. Maybe he was feeding me a line, but he made it damn believable. I held the corkscrew out to him, and he tucked one of the bottles under his arm so he could take it.

Our fingers touched, and I asked, "Who's Addison?"

He winced, like the name was painful. "My ex."

"Was the breakup recent?"

He nodded, sorrow darkening his expression.

I understood the look. I didn't know his story, but I felt the same kind of pain he was trying to hide, and so I said, "Life fucking sucks sometimes. It will strip you bare and throw everything it has at you because it doesn't give a shit what you can handle. It doesn't wait for you to pull yourself together. Some days all we can do is tread water and hope that one day our feet will find solid ground."

He gaped at me, the sorrow gone from his expression. "That might be the most depressing thing anyone has ever said to me."

I gave him a bashful smile because I shouldn't have said it, but I didn't regret it either. "It's my truth, but then again, I'm not in the best headspace right now."

After what she had said, I'd say her headspace was pretty fucked, but then again, I wasn't in great shape myself. Maybe that's why I was so drawn to her. Maybe her broken heart called to mine. I realized I was staring at her too long and told myself to say something. Anything. Oliver, just open your mouth and say something. "Do you like Pink Moscato?"

"It's okay," she said hesitantly, most likely doubting my intentions.

Her eyes were trying to see through me. Long lashes framed her expressive brown eyes—eyes that spoke to me, whispering dark secrets that I was desperate to know.

"Care to join me?" Did I want her to join me? Part of me hoped she would turn me down. "Drinking alone makes me feel pathetic," I added, trying way too hard. Maybe I should've taken the offer from that girl earlier. Rebound sex. That's what you're supposed to do after a breakup, right?

"Let me see your wallet," she finally answered.

"What?"

"Your wallet," she repeated.

"Are you mugging me?"

She rolled her eyes. "All I need is your driver's license."

I tried to hide my smile. "It's in my room. Give me a second."

I ran into my hotel room like a fucking teenaged boy excited about a pretty girl. I set the bottles down on the dresser and grabbed my license. She was waiting for me in her doorway. I handed it to her, saying, "As you requested."

She looked at it before saying, "Okay, Oliver Riser, I'm going to take a picture and send it to my best friend so if I come up missing or dead, she'll know who killed me."

I tried not to smirk as she took the picture, and at the same time, I worried if this was what dating was like these days. Were people always so scared?

"Done," she said, handing it back to me.

"Shall we?" I said, gesturing to my door.

She grabbed her room key, but asked, "Is it cold in your room?"

Fuck. Maybe I liked to torture myself because I knew I would be better off if she put a sweater on, or maybe a snow-suit, but I didn't want her covering herself. That dress was sexy as hell. It wasn't skintight or super short, but the black dress was backless with thin straps that held the knee-length dress in place while the loose flowing fabric hinted at what was beneath. And I was reasonably sure she wasn't wearing a bra. She was trying to kill me. Even standing there talking to her I was rocking a partial.

"I'll turn it up if you're cold," I offered.

"Okay," she said, closing her door and stepping toward me.

Before I let her into my room, I said, "I don't need your license, but knowing your name would be nice."

She smiled, perfect dimples dotting her cheeks as she said, "I'm Willa."

"Just Willa?" I asked.

Her face fell, and I felt like an asshole even though it was a perfectly reasonable question. Before she could answer, I said, "Willa. I like it. It's kind of like Cher or Madonna or Beyoncé. It's powerful."

Her face brightened, and she smiled.

I held out my hand, mostly because I was dying to touch her. As we shook, I said, "Willa, it's nice to meet you. My name is Oliver, but everyone calls me Oli."

"Nice to meet you, Oliver," she returned with a little smirk.

God, she was cute. My hand dwarfed hers, and I liked how different she was from Addison. Addison had big hands. They weren't manly or anything, she just had long fingers. Long and lean like the rest of her. Damn it! I didn't want to think about Addison right now. It wasn't fair that I compared everything to her.

Willa pulled her hand from mine, and I realized again that I was just standing there.

"She must have really fucked with your head," she commented without judgment.

"Let's drink," I said beaming, before turning around and holding the door open for her. She walked through and went to make herself at home. I had two queen beds in my room, whereas she had a single king. It was clear what bed I had slept in, so she went to the other. She sat at the end of the bed, taking in the room.

"Would you like the tour?" I asked.

She laughed, but said, "That would be lovely."

"Alright, over here we have my bed. This is where I've done most of my drinking alone and wallowing. Then over here," I pointed at the table by the windows, "this is where I eat alone. And here," I gestured to the bathroom, "this is where I take long showers and pretend my life isn't in shambles. But over here," I reached down to the mini-refrigerator and opened the door, "this is my favorite part."

She looked in the fridge filled with bottles of Pink Moscato. Then she turned and looked at the table where five more bottles sat and then to the dresser where the two from earlier were sitting.

"Why the hell do you have so much wine?"

"Nope," I shook my head as I turned to grab the bottles on the dresser. "You can't ask me questions like that until I've had a drink or two." I used her corkscrew to open one of the bottles. "Do you always travel with a corkscrew?"

"Most of the time," she said with a shrug. "My friend and I have gone on a few girl's trips, and we realized after the second time forgetting a corkscrew that we should each have one that lives in our suitcase. She and I both have them now. I'm really not an alcoholic. I usually don't drink unless I'm on vacation."

"Is that why you're here? Are you on vacation?"

She shook her head. "No. I'm just running away."

"From what?"

She shook her head. "I will need a drink or two before I answer that one." She stared at the floor, and I knew that look. I had felt it myself. Before she went to a dark place, I handed her a bottle.

She took it but looked confused. "Are there glasses?"

"You're holding it. I don't have glasses, but even if you don't finish that bottle, it's okay. I have more."

"So, we're just drinking from the bottle," she said grinning.

"Yep." I tapped my bottle against hers. "Cheers."

"Cheers," she repeated. She combed a hand through her hair, pushing it back as if she needed it out of the way before she started drinking. I hated how adorable it was.

I sat down on the other bed and faced her. She scooched, so she was directly in front of me. For a while, we drank in silence.

"You know it's even sadder drinking alone when you're drinking directly from the bottle," she said.

I nodded, knowing just how pathetic I was, and yet here she was helping to lessen the pain. "What was your first impression of me?" I asked.

She tilted her head. "You want the honest answer?"

I nodded and took another drink.

It took her a moment to pull her words together, but finally, she said, "I thought you were hot, but I also thought you were probably a tool—a wannabe hipster in your pastel clothes and backpack. I thought . . ." she stopped herself, shaking her head.

"Go on, say it."

"You were holding one of these." She held up her bottle. "I hated how confident you looked holding your pink wine. I concluded you were only that confident because you had a girl up here waiting for you."

"Wow, you thought all of that?"

"I have a lot of thoughts," she replied, relaxing back into

the bed with her legs crossed in front of her. "What was your first impression of me?"

I winced. I should've seen that question coming, but I was too busy thinking about her.

"That good, huh?" she said sarcastically.

I rubbed at the stubble on my chin while I tried to come up with something. I gazed over at her while I thought up a lie.

She smiled at me, and those fucking dimples made an appearance. "No bullshit," she said as if seeing my thoughts. "That's what we're doing, right? The honest truth, even if it's ugly. That's what I'll give you, but only if you reciprocate."

I blew out a breath and told her the truth. "I thought you would be a good rebound."

Her eyebrows went up in surprise. "You thought I'd be a good lay."

I grimaced, saying, "I'm gonna sound like a cocky asshole."

"Honest, ugly truth," she reminded me.

"I get hit on a lot. I never acted on any of those offers because I was with Addison. So, when I saw you in your skimpy cutoff shorts and tight tank, I thought you might be one of those girls who would be interested in a fling."

She laughed. "You thought I was a slut."

"I don't anymore," I blurted.

"I'm not offended. Those shorts are too short, but they're comfy, and I was driving all day. Oh my God, were you hitting on me in the elevator?"

"I was putting out feelers. I'm usually funny, but everything I said just seemed to piss you off."

She sighed. "I was a bitch to you. It's my defense mechanism, and I wanted to push you away because I was attracted to you. I also thought you were here to meet up with your mistress for a midweek hookup."

"You thought so highly of me," I said, trying not to focus on the part where she said she was attracted to me.

"I told you my head isn't in a good place. I tend to expect the worst of people because then it won't hurt so much when they let me down."

It took everything in me not to get up and wrap her in a hug. I knew I couldn't trust myself not to kiss her, and that's not what we were doing here. I needed something to make her less attractive. "Tell me an honest, ugly truth."

"I turned my TV up and slept with earplugs because I was so afraid of hearing sex noises from you and the mistress I thought you were sleeping with."

I laughed because her truth did nothing to lessen her appeal. If anything, it made her more attractive.

Her phone started ringing, and she looked down at it. A groove appeared between her eyebrows as she bit her lip. She glanced at me, saying, "I just need to see what she wants." She stood up as she answered.

She walked away from me, giving me a great view of her exposed back. God, that dress. She had a small tattoo of a bird below her right shoulder blade. I wanted to kiss it. Preferably while I had her bent over the bed and I was buried deep inside of her. I readjusted myself, trying to hide the part of me that was too excited. This was torture. I needed something to cool me down, like a cold shower or a bucket of ice.

Willa spun around, her eyes wide and accusing. She glared at me while she listened to whoever was on the phone.

She lifted her bottle and chugged the rest of her drink before setting it too harshly on the desk. "Okay," she said, "thanks, Jodi."

She hung up, and the silence stretched for a moment. "You're getting married this weekend!"

A bucket of ice water would have been kinder. How the hell did she find out?

I wanted him to deny it so I could throw the proof in his face, and how messed up was that? As soon as Jodi received the photo of his license, she started looking into him. You didn't exactly have to be a detective to find things out about people these days. Thank you, social media.

My phone dinged, and I looked down at the photo Jodi sent me. I let out a short laugh because his fiancée wasn't just beautiful. She was stunning. She was long and willowy with blonde hair and blue eyes. She had flawless fair skin and reeked of wealth. She was everything I wasn't, and Oliver was smiling in the photo. Of course, he was smiling! He held Miss America in his arms.

I didn't notice him move until he was standing over my shoulder. He looked down at the phone in my palm. His hand cradled mine while he moved closer to inspect the photo. I looked up, watching his expression morph into something resembling despair. His jaw tensed as he attempted to hold it together. My anger vanished as a tear landed on my exposed shoulder. I gave him the phone, so I could spin around to face him. He was so much taller than me. I craned my neck to look at him while my hand went to his jaw, my thumb wiping away another tear.

"Tell me," I requested softy.

"We broke up." He threw my phone onto the bed and wiped his face, looking to the ceiling. "I'm fucking pathetic."

"You're human," I said. "We're all pathetic."

He laughed a little, and then he wrapped his arms around me, pulling me against him. His head came down on top of mine, and I discovered how much I loved hugs from Oliver. My arms reciprocated, and after a moment, his fingers traced a line up my back, stopping right over my tattoo.

I stepped back out of his arms. "I don't want to be your rebound," I said.

He shook his head. "I don't either."

I felt rejected, even though he was repeating my words. But I only said it because I can't do meaningless sex, especially not with him. I was already developing feelings for him even as I begged myself not to. I must have given myself away because he went on to explain, "You aren't the rebound type. You're the kind of woman some lucky bastard marries and has lots of babies with."

His words cut me open, and I shook my head, avoiding his eyes. "No, I'm not."

He tilted my chin up, saying, "You are. He just didn't know what he had."

"He knew," I said, pain lancing my heart.

"Then he's an idiot."

"I'm not ready to talk about me yet," I pleaded with him.

My phone chimed, and I realized Jodi was probably

freaking out that he had killed me for learning his secret. I crawled onto his bed to retrieve the phone and sent a quick text. When I turned around, he was sitting down next to me. His back was against the headboard with his legs out in front of him. I mimicked him, sitting with a little gap between us.

I grabbed the bottle in his hand, noticing it was nearly empty, and searched for the alcohol content. I handed it back to him, laughing. "We may as well be drinking grape juice. For a moment, I worried that my tolerance had stepped up."

I climbed off the bed to grab two bottles from the fridge. I uncorked them both, handing one to Oliver before sitting beside him. I could have gone back to the other bed, but it didn't feel right. I enjoyed being close to him.

Oliver held his new bottle out, swirling it. "Addison doesn't actually like wine, but her friends do, so she found a juice that passed for wine so she would fit in."

I look down at my drink. "So, this is Addison's Pink Moscato we're drinking?"

"It is. We were getting married at her grandparent's farm, so we bought all our alcohol ahead of time. The day I picked up the Pink Moscato was the same day she confessed to cheating on me. I forgot the cases were still in the back of my truck when I took off. Of course, it couldn't have been the bourbon. It had to be the Pink fucking Moscato."

I held up my bottle to his, saying, "Here's to Pink fucking Moscato."

He laughed, his eyes sparkling with mirth as he tapped his bottle to mine. I was glad I could do that for him—make him smile on one of the worst days of his life.

"You know," I said, "if it were the bourbon in your truck, you and I wouldn't have met because you don't need a corkscrew to open bourbon. You probably would've been passed out in this room all by yourself."

He didn't laugh this time, and when I looked over at him, his head was resting against the headboard with his face tilted toward me. He reached out, his thumb caressing my lower lip. Before he leaned in to kiss me and I did something stupid like kiss him back, I asked, "She told you she was cheating on you the week you were supposed to get married?"

He dropped his hand, looking defeated. "Exactly a week. She told me Saturday. We're supposed to get married this coming Saturday. She said the guilt was eating at her. She said she loved me and still wanted to get married, but she couldn't go into it without telling me. She said things just went too far. She said it only happened a handful of times over the years and that it will never happen again."

I scoff. "Oh, well, if it's only a handful of times then I guess it's okay to be unfaithful."

He shook his head. "Honestly, I love her enough that I think I would've let it go, but . . ."

He said, *love her*. Not he used to love her. He still loved her. I reminded myself not to let him kiss me. He was not allowed to kiss me when he still loved her.

I realized he wasn't talking and tried to remember what he said last. When I remembered, I asked, "You would've let it go, but what?"

"It's so fucking cliché," he muttered.

"Ahh," I said, the alcohol loosening my tongue. "Did she fuck your best friend or your brother?"

"I don't have a brother."

I grimaced. I wanted to be wrong. I can't imagine if I caught Evan with Jodi. It would have destroyed me.

He scoffed. "And it's not like he's only my buddy from work. Travis has been my best friend since we were three and our parents made our playdates. He may as well have been my brother. He was in every way that mattered.

"And Addie and I have been together since we were seventeen. She always said we were High school sweethearts till the end of time. Eleven years is a long time. Sometimes I was tempted by other girls, but I never acted. Travis encouraged me to have one-night stands all the time in college. He said I just needed to get it out of my system, and now I wonder if it's because he felt guilty. She wouldn't tell me when it started between them, but she said they hadn't been together since we got engaged."

"Your best friend and your girl. That's cold. Did you confront him after she told you?"

He took a long swig before confessing. "There are some things you can't take back, you know. I didn't want to do something or say something I couldn't take back. You always hear how people catch their significant other cheating and feel this murderous rage. I didn't feel that. I felt humiliated and hurt. And more than anything I wanted to know why. Why would they do this? It happens once, it's an accident, but it kept happening, Willa. Why? What did he have that I didn't? And was it that important to him that he'd risk our friendship? Was it just sex, or was it more? What if he's in love with her? Or worse, what if she's in love with him?"

"Don't you think you're giving them too much credit? In my experience, men like beautiful unavailable women because they're forbidden. What's more forbidden than your best friend's girlfriend?"

He swung his gaze to me. "You have a very low opinion of people."

"How do you not?" I argued. "People do shitty things to each other all the time."

"I don't."

I rolled my eyes. "You may not realize you do, but I'm sure you do."

"No, I don't."

I leaned against him, feeling the alcohol loosening my reservations. "Oliver, nobody is perfect. Not even you."

There was humor in his voice. "Is that grape juice kicking in?"

I closed my eyes and nodded against him.

He nudged me with his shoulder, and I lifted up as he jumped off the bed. "We need music," he announced as he practically bounced on his heels.

"What?" I asked, wondering where all his sudden energy came from.

"Come on. I'm putting you to sleep with my depressing stories. I didn't ask you here so you could listen to me cry all night. Do you have music on your phone?"

I'm already crawling to the edge of the bed to join him. "Where's your phone?"

"I left it in my truck, so I wouldn't be tempted to call her."

I pulled up my music and handed the phone to him. He scrolled through my music, judging me, I'm sure.

"Workout mix. What's this?"

"Eh..." I responded before the hardcore rap blared from the speaker.

He laughed and I ripped my phone from his hands to play my pop station. If he wanted to dance, then we would dance. I went old school with Spice Girls because when I was young, Jodi and I created a whole dance routine to the song "Wannabe". I was suddenly dying to show him. Okay, so I was definitely a little drunk.

"Oliver, I'm gonna need you to step back off the dance floor while I show you how true professionals do it." I shooed him out of the small space and back toward the bed as "Wannabe" came on.

He sat back with his eyes glued to me. I handed him my drink and began my dance routine. We were maybe seven-years-old when we choreographed this dance, so unless we were child prodigies, the dance was really as bad as I thought it was. I looked to Oliver, who was barely containing his laughter.

"You want the honest, ugly truth?" I asked him.

"Always," he responded.

"I'm not a good dancer and my friend and I are not child prodigies." I swung my hips and nearly toppled over.

In a flash, his hands were on me. It was an overreaction, but I was not going to push him away. Instead, I rested my hands on his shoulders while his hands were on my back. He slid them down, placing them in the small of my back. He pulled me forward until I was against him, and then he started swaying. And that's how we ended up slow dancing to "Wannabe."

I rested my cheek against his chest so I wouldn't be so

tempted to lift up and kiss him because even if I was a little drunk; I remembered he still loved Addison.

His mouth came to my ear to whisper, "Better not get with my friends."

I tilted my head up, my lips a breath from his. "Who said I wanted to be your lover?"

His nose touched mine, and my eyes fell closed expectantly because my body is a traitor. But he didn't kiss me. The prickly scruff on his jaw rubbed against my cheek, and his mouth was back at my ear. "Your body told me. And the truth is I really fucking want to kiss you."

The song ended, but we kept swaying, holding one another because the moment we let go, our instincts would take over. Our desires were stronger than our logic.

I reached deep down, remembering the look on Evan's face when I walked in on him and Estelle in our bed together. For the rest of my life, I will remember the look he gave me because I expected to find panic or fear, but what I saw was relief. Relief that he didn't have to hide anymore. Relief that he could move on with his life and be done with me. His relief is what hurt the most.

I pushed away from Oliver, spinning away from him to take a few steps before I said, "You love Addison. She hurt you, but you're still in love with her, and I won't be the other woman."

I turned to face him from across the room. He wasn't looking at me. His hands were on his hips, and his head hung forward while his muscled chest rose and fell with each breath he took. I watched him for a while before asking, "Should I leave?"

He looked up at me then, panic in his big blue eyes. That

was the panic I was looking for from Evan. Oliver didn't look relieved that I was giving him an out. He swallowed. "Do you want to leave?" he asked.

"No, but I'm afraid we'll do something we both regret."

He looked serious as he said, "I just have one more song I want us to dance to, and if you still want to leave after that, I won't stop you."

I opened my mouth to speak, hesitant because I didn't know if I could do this, but Oliver didn't wait for my response. The song started playing, and my eyes shot to him, a slow smile creeping across my face until I was smiling like a lunatic. "I know I don't have this on my playlist!"

"Well, now, you do," he said, beaming at me from across the room as the accordion music played. He stepped forward reaching his hand out for me, asking, "May I have this dance?"

I rolled my eyes and took his hand, saying, "You continue to surprise me, Oliver."

Then we danced the hell out of the "Chicken Dance".

5

My whole life people had called me Oli, and I loved that she refused to shorten my name. We hooked arms and swung around in circles as the "Chicken Dance" demanded. I watched her thick hair flow out behind her in dark waves. I laughed because she looked overjoyed, and it filled me with this euphoric sensation. We were good together. I might not know her past, but I couldn't imagine anything she could tell me to make me dislike her. I wished we had met at a different time, under different circumstances because neither of us were in a good place. I knew enough to know that was a poor way to start a new relationship, and I wasn't interested in a rebound. I wanted her.

She was facing me, laughing as the music sped up and she went through the motions so quickly they all bled together. Then we were back arm in arm, and I couldn't remember the last time I was so happy.

Once the song finished, she collapsed back onto the bed,

laying on her back with her arms sprawled out to the sides while she caught her breath. "I don't know the last time I laughed so hard," she said to the ceiling. "Thank you for that, Oliver. I needed it."

"I think we both did," I said, sitting on the other bed.

She lifted to her elbow to look at me. "You are my favorite stranger."

"I'm not a stranger. I'm just a new arrival."

She grinned at me, saying, "Are you? Or are you just visiting?"

God, I hoped not. "I don't know."

She sprang off the bed, and rushed to the bathroom, saying, "Bathroom break!"

Once she reemerged, it was my turn because two bottles of wine is too much for one bladder.

She sat up straighter when I came out of the bathroom. Crossing her legs, she asked, "Do you think you'll get back together with Addison?"

I sat across from her, wanting to say no, because sitting here with Willa, I couldn't imagine going back to Addison, but the truth was, I didn't know. "I don't know," I said. "We've been together for so long that being with her has become a reflex. She's part of my routine. Like last night when I laid down, I wanted to call her and tell her good-night. I've been so tempted to look at my phone that I left it in the truck so I wouldn't cave."

"Does anyone know where you are?"

"No. I didn't know where I was going. I just drove until I felt like stopping. I had to go shopping once I got here because I didn't pack anything."

"Have you talked to anyone?" she asked.

"No."

"Oliver! They're probably worried sick about you. You need to tell someone."

"I mean, Addison kinda knows."

"What did you tell her?"

"That I needed time."

Her eyes widened. "Is that all you said?"

"Basically." I didn't remember my exact words because at the time I had been blinded by her confession. I was too focused on escaping before I lost my dinner—the dinner she made me in preparation of bad news. Not even a mile from our house, I had to pull over on the road to get sick.

When I snapped out of my thoughts, I noticed Willa was gawking at me. "What?" I asked, feeling defensive.

She shook her head and swallowed. "Oliver, saying you need time is not the same as saying I'm breaking up with you. Does she even understand that you're not together? Does she know you called off the wedding?"

I shrugged. "Yeah, I think so."

She stood. "Oliver!"

I sat up straighter. "What?"

"Saying you need time is not the equivalent to saying you can't marry her!"

"She knew what I meant," I said to vindicate myself.

Her hands landed on her hips. "Did she?"

I started to second guess myself.

Willa ran her hands through her hair and turned away from me, exasperated.

I drove away from Addison late Saturday evening. Today

was Tuesday, and it had been a few days since I talked to anyone. I stood, saying, "Could I borrow your phone to call my dad?"

She practically threw her phone at me.

I dialed my dad's number and waited as it rang. It was almost eleven and I wasn't sure if he would answer. "Hello."

"Hey, dad."

"Hey, you getting excited about your big day?"

Fuck! I gripped a hand in my hair, trying to refrain from shouting obscenities. Instead, I looked to Willa who was biting her nails, looking both worried and cute as hell.

Focus!

"Dad, eh . . ." I squeezed my eyes closed and gritted my teeth. What the hell was I supposed to say? "Dad, let me call you back." Before he could say anything, I hung up.

I was so angry that I couldn't see straight. I started dialing Addison and Willa ripped the phone from my hand just as I was about to hit send. "You're not calling her from my number." She typed something in and handed the phone back to me. "Here, it'll show up as a blocked call."

I hit send, and Addison answered right away.

"Addison." My voice was cold. I had never spoken to her this way. It hurt. It hurt me to be mean to her.

"Oli, Oh my God!" she sobbed. "I was so worried about you. Where are you?"

"Addison, why does my dad think we're still getting married this weekend?"

She gasped. "Oli, you don't mean that."

I heard Travis in the background, and suddenly I was furious. This was the rage people felt when they discovered their significant other was cheating. Maybe it was just a delayed response. "You've gotta be fucking kidding me, Addison. He's there with you right now?"

"Umm . . ." she hesitated. "Yeah, but only because we were both so worried about you."

"Worried about me?" I shook my head. "Fuck, Addison. Cancel the goddamn wedding. I can't marry you."

"Oli," she sobbed, breaking my heart.

"Oli," Travis said, coming on the line. "It's not what you think."

"Fuck you, Travis!" I hung up and went to chuck the phone across the room. I stopped myself just in time, remembering it was Willa's phone. My heart was racing, and I really wanted to throw something. Instead, I tossed the phone onto the mattress and laced my fingers together on top of my head, shouting, "What the fuck?"

Willa's sweet voice broke through my fury. "Wanna go break something?"

My eyes shot to her.

She smiled mischievously, waggling her eyebrows at me. "Come on. It'll be fun."

She didn't wait for a response as she grabbed her phone and room key. She marched out the door and waited for me in the hall. She was such a mystery. I felt like I'd known her forever, but I knew nothing about her, and I really wanted to remedy that. I grabbed my key and followed her. She led me into her hotel room, saying, "I'm so glad I brought them with me."

"Brought what with you?"

"You'll see." She grabbed her purse, and then we were right back out the door.

"Where are we going?" I asked as I went along with her down the hall.

After hitting the button for the elevator, she leaned against the wall, her body swaying to the side. She laughed at herself, and it was intoxicating.

"It's possible that I'm having a delayed reaction to that wine," she said.

I smirked. "You think?"

She shrugged. "It's a possibizzle."

The doors dinged open, and she spun to board the elevator. She stood against the back wall, watching as I pressed the button for the lobby.

With a coy grin, she said, "Honest truth. The first time we rode this elevator together, I was so nervous and distracted by you that I forgot to hit the button."

My eyes slid down to the hem of her dress, but I was picturing the shorts she wore the day before. "Truth," I said. "I really liked your shorts."

Her index finger touched her lips as she tried to stifle a smile. I stared at those lips, wanting them more than I wanted to break something. I stepped towards her just as the elevator doors opened to a busy lobby.

I smiled as if I wasn't just about to kiss her, but she knew. She threaded her fingers through mine and led me through the lobby and out to the parking lot. Her car was an older Toyota Camry, and for a moment, I worried she would try to drive. But she stopped at her trunk, opening the compartment. There seemed to be a lot of random things inside.

As an explanation, she said, "I still have a lot of things in here from the move."

I didn't know what move she was talking about, but I

nodded like I understood because I didn't want to risk making her sad. She bent over to reach a box deep in her trunk, and her dress rose up her thighs.

There I was, staring at her ass when she peeked back over her shoulder. She lifted an eyebrow and said, "Maybe instead of ogling me, you could lift this heavy box that I can barely reach."

"Can't I do both?"

She stood up and pointed at the box. I reached in and grabbed it, realizing she wasn't joking about its weight. "What's in here?"

She smiled. "These are plates Evan and I bought together."

"Who is Evan?"

She seemed surprised I didn't know. "My ex-husband," she said, rolling her eyes.

There it was. The baggage that weighed her down and made her feel like she was barely treading water. Evan had turned her into this jaded woman who had lost her faith in men. I hated Evan.

She grabbed a thick linen bag. It looked like the bag Santa carried, except more durable. I had no idea where one would find such a thing or why they would need it, but Willa was full of surprises.

She looked up at me as she flung the empty bag over her shoulder and slammed her trunk. She asked, "Why are you laughing?"

"Where did you get that bag?"

"Don't mock my bag. Come on," Willa said, looking around as if she didn't know where she was leading me. Maybe she didn't. I was pretty sure she was making things up as she went, but I still followed her.

"This way." She led me to the far end of the parking lot, towards a gas station right off the highway exit ramp. Over here, the freeway noises were more prominent, and the lights were faint. It was a place I would never want her to hang out alone.

She turned, saying, "You can set the box down."

As soon as the box was on the ground, she was ripping it open to pull out a stack of white ceramic plates. She emptied the box, setting all the dishes on the ground except for two which she loaded into her Santa bag. She tightened the cords at the top, closing the bag. Hefting it onto her shoulder, she took a few steps away. Then she swung the bag over her shoulder with all the strength she possessed. It slammed against the pavement, and I heard the sound of shattering glass over the freeway noises. Willa smiled, looking satisfied. Then she repeated the action over and over, until the bag hung limp, all the glass shattered but contained.

She walked the bag back to me with a smile. After emptying the shards into the cardboard box, she handed the bag to me with an encouraging grin. "Allow yourself to feel all the anger and pain and then let it go."

I nodded, following her example, smashing the plates until there was nothing but tiny shards. Even emptying the bag felt therapeutic, like I was pouring out all my problems. And surprisingly it wasn't just Addison cheating on me. It was all the things I had been suppressing for so many years.

It was the time I gave up my career so Addison could go to medical school. It was the fact that she refused to marry me until she was stable in her career. I didn't realize how much of my life I changed to fit her. I never even told her how I felt. I never fought for myself because I was so convinced that she was the best thing that had ever happened to me. I was whipped, and she never demanded it. I just did it, because . . . well, because it was Addison, and I loved her. But I was so busy admiring her that I overlooked the fact that I wasn't happy.

Willa and I took turns, back and forth, until the plates were all destroyed. We didn't speak. I was too busy processing, and she didn't push me for my thoughts.

My head was spinning over all the things I hadn't noticed before. Now that I was looking from a different perspective, I didn't know how I had been so blind. Understanding the severity of my loss made me feel heavier. I hadn't just lost Addison. I had lost the last eleven years by living for someone else. I gave up my own goals to follow hers. The weight of the last eleven years shifted into something more substantial.

I couldn't marry Addison even if she hadn't been unfaithful. Knowing what I know now, I'm almost thankful she cheated. It just sucked that it was with Travis.

"What are you thinking?" Willa asked.

"I just realized I let Addison control my life. I'm relieved we aren't getting married." The weight seemed to fall away as I spoke those words. I was free but grieving my life, my love, my friendship. I didn't feel whole, but at least I was free.

I was grateful Willa didn't respond because I didn't think I could explain all that I meant. I picked up the box, asking, "Do you want to keep this?"

She shook her head no, and I walked off, carrying it to

the gas station dumpster. I folded the top together to better contain the glass before disposing of it.

When I met back up with Willa, I collided with her body, pulling her in for a hug. She reciprocated, and I kissed her temple, whispering, "Thank you, Willa. I'm so happy I got stuck with the Pink fucking Moscato."

6

WILLA

$\mathcal{E}$verything he did affected me, and as he whispered in my ear, I'm pretty sure he was really thanking me and not copping a feel. The hug was genuine and platonic for him. For me, it sent a fire straight to my lady parts. Maybe I was just feeling revved up because I just released so much pent up anger by breaking those ugly plates, but I had to make a mental note not to gyrate against him.

Dear Lord, help me. I don't remember feeling this out of control with Evan, ever, not even in the very beginning.

Crazy ideas about love and destiny started playing in my head, and I did my best to squash them. I pulled away from him before I did anything stupid, and we started back toward the hotel. We made a pit stop by my car to drop off the bag. As I was closing the trunk, Oliver said, "I'm not ready to go back inside."

I could tell he was still sorting through some stuff in his head. I lifted myself to sit on the trunk, saying, "It's a nice night." I patted the spot next to me.

He eyed the car. "I don't think that's good for your car."

I shrugged. "My car is a piece of shit. I should've gotten a new one a year ago, but I'm sentimental about this damn car. Now get your ass up here."

He slid up to sit next to me, saying, "If you insist."

We sat there for a moment. The sound from the highway was more subdued over here, reminding me of white noise. Oliver laid back, his back resting against my rear window. I tried to do the same but didn't like the feel of the glass against the bare skin of my back. As I sat up, Oliver pulled me into him, tucking me into his side with my head resting against his chest while he looked up into the night sky.

Lying there with Oliver's arm around me felt like the most natural thing in the world.

"Do you think everything happens for a reason?" he asked.

I shrugged against him. "Yes and no. I don't believe in fate, but I believe that most of the time we have the opportunity to decide what we do with the cards we're dealt."

"I thought I understood my life, but now I can't seem to make sense of things that used to make perfect sense to me."

"We all think we see the world as it is, but the truth is, we are all living in our own little glass bubbles, and when we look out at the world, we are looking through a pane of glass that has been tainted by our past experiences and current situations."

"Why did you divorce your husband?" he asked out of the blue.

"I didn't." There was shame in my admission. "He divorced me after I found him in our bed with another woman."

I felt him move, lifting his head to look down at me. I didn't move, and eventually, he relaxed, but the arm that was around me shifted so his hand could pull the hair from my face.

I expected him to say words of sympathy, but instead, he asked, "Would you have divorced him if he hadn't beaten you to it?"

"I don't know. I was in a terrible place at the time. I could barely get out of bed, let alone pull myself together enough to file for divorce. Eventually, I suppose I would have."

"What do you do for a living?" he asked in a sudden topic change.

"I'm a teacher."

He scoffed. "Really?"

I lifted up on my elbow, offended. Looking down at him, I said, "Yes, really."

"What do you teach?"

"Right now, I'm helping with high school special education."

"No shit?"

I relaxed, laying my head against him and shifted the conversation. "What do you do?"

"I'm in commercial real estate."

"Hmm. So, are you missing work this week?"

"I mostly make my own schedule, but I already had this week blocked off because of the wedding."

"Do you like what you do?"

"It's okay. It made the most financial sense while Addison was still in school and through her residency, but now, I might look into something else. I don't know. I guess I should make one life-altering decision at a time."

"Addison is a doctor?"

"Pediatric oncologist."

"Damn," I said. I didn't mean to say it out loud, but it slipped out. Quietly, I added, "You know that makes it a little harder to hate her, right?"

"Oh, I'm aware." He sighs. "That's just it. She's not a bad person. She's one of the best people I know. She's easy to love because she gives so freely. Every opportunity I got, I would bend over backward to lighten her load. I didn't realize I was doing it. We were comfortable in our relationship, like roommates that had sex. We never fought. And I took that to mean things were going well. But we were missing the emotion a relationship like ours should have had."

"Would you have married her if she didn't confess to cheating?"

"Absolutely, because I didn't see any of this. Not until you." His fingers ran the length of my arm, chased by goosebumps. As he ran his fingers back up, he asked, "Are you cold?"

"No, I'm okay." The truth was, I was kind of cold, and it had to be creeping close to one in the morning, but I wasn't ready for the night to be over.

"What does the bird on your back symbolize?" he asked, tracing it with his finger.

"What makes you think it symbolizes something. Maybe I just thought it was cute."

"Did you?"

"No."

"You don't strike me as the type of person to put something on your body just because it's cute. I'm sure it has a purpose."

"If you laugh at me, I will murder you."

"You think I would laugh at something that's so meaningful to you."

I sighed before beginning, "Growing up we had this dog. I got her as a puppy on my eighth birthday. She was my favorite thing in the world. I even liked her more than my friend, Jodi. I didn't have any siblings, so naturally, I treated this dog like she was my sister. We went everywhere together. I would even have pretend-fights with her because I knew siblings fought sometimes. She meant the world to me.

"I always slept on my stomach, and she would sleep next to me with her head resting just below my right shoulder blade." I touched the location of the tattoo. "She lived to be thirteen, which is a long time for a German Shepherd. She died on my twenty-first birthday, and I got the tattoo as a way to commemorate her." I sniffled. "Damn, I haven't cried about her in years."

As I wiped away my tears, he said, "That's beautiful. I just have one follow-up question. If it commemorates your dog, why is it a bird?"

"Her name was Birdie."

There was humor in his voice as he asked, "You named your dog Birdie?"

"Yes, I did, and now I have to kill you. I told you not to laugh."

"I'm not laughing," he said, squeezing me. He pressed a

kiss on the top of my head. "I swear I wasn't laughing at you. I think it's perfect. I love the way your mind works."

I didn't know what to say to that, so I laid there, relaxing into his warmth. Twelve hours ago, he was a stranger. How could I feel so comfortable wrapped up in his arms?

The next thing I knew, Oliver was saying my name, "Willa. Willa, wake up. We have to go in. You're freezing."

I couldn't believe I fell asleep on him. "I'm sorry."

"Don't be sorry. I would've let you sleep there all night, but you started shivering."

As soon as I sat up, Oliver slipped off the car and turned to help me down as if I were incapable of doing it on my own. The feminist in me balked at the move, while the rest of me loved sliding down his body. I would take that 'help' anytime.

There was tension between us that hadn't been their earlier. I got the sense he had sorted his demons, and no longer wanted to keep things platonic. I wasn't about to fight him and therein lied the problem. I promised myself I would not have sex with him no matter how much my body demanded it.

He wrapped his arm around my shoulder as we walked toward the hotel. A limo pulled up just as we were entering the building. The limo doors opened, and a group of rowdy girls in their early twenties came stumbling out. I glanced back to see they were all decked out in bachelorette party attire. Their slurred words and overly affectionate behavior made it obvious they were drunk. They linked arms, leaning on each other for support, which was dangerous because they were all unstable, teetering around in their stilettos. It was a miracle their mini-dresses weren't showing more than they should.

"Wait," I said, and Oliver paused, but I pulled him forward, continuing my thought. "It's Tuesday. Who has a bachelorette party on a Tuesday?"

He pushed the button for the elevator, saying, "You know what they say about going to the club on a Tuesday."

I laughed aloud, leaning into him. "You think they're choosey?"

"You got the reference."

"Of course, I know that song." I peeked over his shoulder, noting, "It looks like we'll be sharing our elevator with them."

"Don't worry, I'll protect you," he whispered in my ear.

"I'm not the one that needs protection," I said to him as the five girls approached, all of them taking him in. I nudged him, whispering, "Here's your chance at sloppy rebound sex."

The doors opened for the seven of us to pile in the elevator.

"Hey there," said one of the girls as she eye-humped Oliver. "Are you two together?"

"Oh, us," I said, pulling away from Oliver's grip. "No. He's my brother."

From the corner of my eye, I saw Oliver's head jerk toward me. I smiled bigger as the girls openly hit on him, one of them stroking her hand down his chest. He tried to fend them off, and eventually, he said, "Sorry, ladies, I only have eyes for my sister." He reached out, his hand cupping my butt to give it a little squeeze. And as if that wasn't enough, he moved me to stand in front of him, using me as a human shield. His lips fell to the crook of my neck, and he kissed me, his tongue sliding across the sensitive skin. He whispered, "Sweet revenge." His breath sent a shock wave of desire through me.

The girls were making faces of disgust as they unloaded from the elevator. They made some snide comments, but I couldn't tell you what they said because I was too focused on Oliver's sweet revenge. The doors closed again, and the elevator rose.

"They're gone," I breathed. "You can move now." Even as I said it, my eyes closed as my head tilted back to rest against his chest, giving him better access.

I felt his silent laugh against my skin as his lips continued to press soft kisses along my neck and shoulder. His breath tickled as he whispered, "Who said I was doing it for them?"

"Oliver." It was a plea, but I didn't know whether I was asking him to stop or insisting he keep going.

"Willa," he replied, nearly breathless.

The elevator dinged, announcing that we had reached our floor, but neither of us moved. I watched the doors close back up, and Oliver's hands slid down my arms, his fingers interlocking with mine. "I want to feel you, Willa. I'm dying to touch you."

Then why was he holding my hands? Oh, right, he had restraint, something I seemed incapable of at the moment. The elevator descended, and his face nestled against my neck as he tried to pull himself together.

Thank God, the teenagers waiting for the elevator were making so much noise, because it gave Oliver and me enough warning to break our connection just before the doors opened to the lobby. I tried to move to stand next to Oliver, but he held me in place, saying to the group of guys, "We're going up."

The group loaded onto the elevator, all of them suddenly much quieter than before as they kept glancing our way. I felt the flush across my cheeks, and I didn't know if Oliver looked disheveled. As my back pressed back into him, I felt the evidence of his arousal and slid against it, causing him to suck in a breath.

The doors to the third floor opened and the guys took off. I stepped forward, looking over my shoulder to inspect the impressive bulge in Oliver's pants.

"You think this is funny?" he asked.

I smiled at him as I backed to the doors, putting my foot in the opening, so we didn't take another unnecessary ride to the lobby. "No," I replied. "I'm just glad I don't get boners when I'm horny."

Oliver adjusted himself, stepping out of the elevator with me. "You think you weren't just as obvious," he said, turning to me and grazing a hand across one of my flushed cheeks. "Pink is a good color on you. And don't think for a second those boys didn't notice the headlights you're sporting." His eyes flicked to my chest, and I crossed my arms, covering my breasts.

He shook his head. "I don't want you to hide from me."

He grabbed my hand and led me to our doors. I stopped before we reached his door because if I went in there with him, I would be too tempted to strip him naked and ride him like a cowgirl. Even the image in my head had me barely containing my desires. I leaned against my door as I turned to face him. "I should get some sleep."

Blue eyes melted me as he stepped in close. He leaned

on my door next to me, gently brushing his fingers through my hair, pushing it back from my face.

"I should probably get some sleep, too," he said softly as he leaned in, staring at my lips. I tilted my chin toward him and the hand that was brushing my hair, wrapped around the back of my neck, pulling me toward him.

His breath teased my lips as he whispered, "Truth. I've never wanted to kiss someone as badly as I want to kiss you right now."

That was my out. That was when I should have pulled away, but instead, I said, "Then do it."

I expected his lips to crush mine in a desperate kiss, but his lips were feather-soft against mine. I had never experienced such a slow sensually agonizing kiss. He was drawing it out as long as he could, and I savored the feel, soaking up every second. He teased my mouth with his tongue, and before I lost my mind, I wrapped my arms around him, pulling him closer, needing more, wanting it all. He finally relented. His plush lips grew demanding, and his tongue found mine. I let out a pleasure moan—like a long, exaggerated porn moan, and instead of thinking it was absurd, he reacted like it was the hottest thing he had ever heard.

Suddenly, my back was pressed up against the door, and he was devouring me. His hands wandered down my body, exploring like he couldn't help himself. His thumb swiped my nipple, and I broke our kiss to get some air. "Oliver," I panted, and he groaned in response. His mouth didn't stop. His lips traveled down to the base of my neck. I noticed that seemed to be his favorite spot. His teeth gently nipped at the skin of my shoulder while his hands grabbed my ass, pressing me against his hard length. I was about to have an orgasm fully dressed right there in the hallway if we continued, and as much as I wanted the release, I knew this was going too far, way too fast.

"Wait," I said, panting.

His hands released my ass, and his palms went to the door behind me as his forehead rested on my shoulder. He was breathing heavily, and I felt like a tease.

"Sorry," I whispered. "I didn't mean to—"

"No." He paused, taking a breath. "I took it too far. You're just so fucking hot."

"But I've only known you for a day. I can't do this."

He pulled back, looking me in the eye. "It feels like so much longer."

My gaze flicked to his lips.

"Stop it," he reprimanded. "It's hard enough not to kiss you."

"God, that kiss," I whispered.

"I know," he agreed. "Willa, I need you to tell me good-night. If you don't, I'm afraid I'll kiss you again."

I grinned because that made me feel all hot and squishy inside. Oliver made me feel desirable and not just for my body. He also told me he loved the way my mind worked. I let go of him, and he dropped his hands in return. "Good-night, Oliver. I have a feeling I'll be seeing you in my dreams tonight."

His eyes blazed at my comment. He slowly shook his head. "Goodnight, Willa. Have sweet dreams and remember the real thing will be so much sweeter." He kissed my nose and stepped back so I could open my door. I scanned my keycard, turned the handle, and push the door open, tempted to pull him in with me so we could finish what we started. As if sensing this, he backed away.

"No, no," he said. "That look leads to trouble, and I never want you to regret me. Goodnight, Willa. Close the door."

I let the door fall closed between us and stood in the entry for a moment. I peeked through the peephole to spy on Oliver. He rested a hand against my door, leaning forward as if he was attempting to pull himself together. I continued to watch him until he pulled away and went into his own room. I heard his door click shut, and I slid down the wall, wondering if tonight was real.

If it was, then I was in trouble.

Willa reclined back in a lounge chair beside the pool. She was tucked back in the shade, too engrossed in the book she was reading to pay attention to anything around her. Kids were screaming with excitement while their parents shouted with exasperation. Music was playing while hordes of teenage baseball players kept looking her way, not even pretending they weren't checking her out. Not that Willa would have noticed their attention.

She wore her sheer white bathing suit cover-up over her black bikini, showing off just enough to let everyone know they wanted to see more. Her large sunglasses made her look like a celebrity in hiding. Her nearly black hair spilled over her shoulders in thick waves.

I didn't want to smother her, but there was no way she would notice me unless I went over and talked to her. I wasn't dressed for the pool. I hadn't been planning to swim, I simply needed to find her, and now that I had, I didn't know what to do with myself.

She didn't even look up as I took the seat next to hers.

She flipped a page and continued reading. Instead of interrupting her as I had planned, I reclined back, waiting for her to notice me. And after about twenty minutes of waiting, I fell asleep.

"—you been there?"

I woke to her voice. Popping my eyes open, I turned to look at her. "Huh?"

Her book sat on the seat next to her as she turned sideways in her chair to face me. "How long have you been there?"

I rubbed my face, still waking up. "I don't know. I came out here around eleven. What time is it now?"

She smiled. "It's one."

"What you're saying is I've been sitting next to you for two hours, and you are just now noticing me."

"I'm really focused when I read, and to be fair; you're a very quiet sleeper."

The way she smiled at me reminded me of the night before, and I had to sit up in my seat before my pants became too tight. I turned to face her, and she looked me over.

"I see you're back to wearing your pink shorts," she said with humor.

I glanced down at my shorts. "I didn't pack for this trip. I only have so many clothes." When I looked back up, she had a sexy gleam in her eye, and I asked, "Willa, are you having dirty thoughts?"

She shrugged with a grin. "Maybe. Do you always wear your hair in a man bun?"

"Most of the time. Why?"

"Just wondering," she said as she gathered her things.

She stood, asking, "Are you hungry? Do you want to get some lunch?"

I stopped myself from saying something vulgar, and said, "Sure. Where are we going?"

"I still need to try those nachos you were raving about."

"Oh." I ran a hand through my hair. "About those nachos."

She gave me a curious look. "What about them?"

"Truth. I haven't eaten at the hotel bar."

"What?" She looked angry. "Why would you lie about something so stupid?"

"Because I had nothing to say, and I needed to say something to you."

"What if I got the nachos and they were terrible?"

"You couldn't. I checked. They don't even have nachos."

She propped her hand on her hip, trying to show attitude she couldn't pull off. Shit, she was even sexier when she was indignant. I attempted to hide my grin as I reached out to caress her jaw. She batted my hand away. "That's the last lie, Oliver."

Oh shit. For someone so petite, she was surprisingly quick. I followed her around the pool. As soon as we were inside, I grabbed her wrist and spun her around. I pinned her to the wall, and she didn't fight me. She just glared at me with tight lips.

"Willa, I'm sorry. I didn't mean to upset you. I lied to you before we started telling our ugly truths."

Her tight lips turned up into a smirk and her hands wrapped around my neck, her fingers splaying in my hair.

"Wait, you're *not* mad?"

She shook her head. "I just wanted to see if you'd chase

me or let me go. This," she said, pressing her body into mine, "was a nice surprise."

I pulled away, forcing her to loosen her grip on me. "I don't like games, Willa."

She stepped forward, pushing up to her tiptoes. Her lips brushed mine, before she said, "Oliver, I like you more than I should, and a big part of me wants to avoid you because I don't know how this could end well. I'm not trying to play games. I'm not. I'm just cynical and—"

I tried to use my words but kissing her took priority. I dipped my head, finding her lips. Her responding moan was a lure, and I was a weak bastard who desperately wanted what she was offering. I wanted to swallow her whole.

She bit my lip, and my fingers gripped her ass. I was about to lift her up against the wall, but someone opened the door, coming in from outside. She broke our kiss, and I had to catch my breath. I didn't give a shit that people were watching us, but she cared.

"Willa." I was pleading, fucking pleading as I lowered my head to her shoulder.

"I don't want to be those people who make out in public," she said, breathless.

I closed my eyes, hoping for some of the control I had last night. Where had it gone?

"Oliver." Her voice was a whisper, and I would do anything she said so long as she used that tone.

I pulled back, giving her space to breathe. She seemed to straighten herself out, and then she grabbed my hand and pulled me toward the lobby. I was hoping she would stop at the bank of elevators and lead me up to her room. I stared longingly at the elevator doors as we passed by.

When she pulled me out through the lobby doors, I asked, "Where are we going?"

"We are going to sit down in a public place and have a meal and talk. I am not some easy girl, but you're making me crazy, and I don't—"

"Willa, you don't have to explain yourself. I get it. And I'm not some one-night stand." I said, putting a hand to my hip. "Nuh-uh, not this guy."

She shoved me, and I lowered my hand to lace it through hers. "Your car or mine?"

"Mine," she said with gusto.

I thought for sure she would pick my truck, but I had no idea how much she loved her car. She broke from my hand so she could dig through her bag to find her keys. She pulled them out and went to the driver's side door.

I ducked down into her car, taking the passenger seat. "Huh, it's spotless. I was expecting it to be as messy as your trunk."

"My trunk is a fluke," she justified, "And the makeup on the dresser. I'm actually a bit OCD."

"I guess I haven't seen this side of you. How obsessive are we talking? Is this a compulsive cleanliness thing, or do you have to flip the light switches sixteen times before you can sleep? Either is fine. I just want to know what I'm dealing with."

The air conditioning came on, blasting us with hot air as she started the car. "I just like my things a certain way," she said, "I like to keep things organized."

"You like control."

She turned with a scowl.

"Am I wrong?" I asked, attempting to hide my smile.

She pursed her lips, looking forward for a moment before answering, "There is so much we can't control."

I grinned. "Is that an admission?"

"That's a fact. Control in itself is an illusion. All we can do is decide how we deal with what we're dealt. I'm not so self-involved as to think I am the center of the universe. There are a million things bigger than me. An asteroid could kill me, or I might get mauled by a rabid squirrel. A bridge could fall on me, or I might get struck by lightning. I can't really prevent a cancer diagnosis or some other horrible disease. There are too many things we can't control, so yeah, I like things neat, and I get to make that decision."

As she backed out of her parking space, I said, "I understand what you're saying, but I feel like if you're making a point, you should've gone bigger than a squirrel. If you're going to be mauled, at least make it a bear, or wolf, maybe a mountain lion."

She drove out of the parking lot, saying, "But those things are already scary. You would know to look out for a bear, wolf, or mountain lion. I mean they make a bear spray to deter bears. I've never seen squirrel spray because squirrels are cute with their fluffy tails and spunky antics. No one would expect to get mauled by a squirrel, but they're technically rodents. They have teeth and claws, and if one bit someone just right, a squirrel could potentially kill someone."

"That's ridiculous!"

She shrugs. "People die from absurd things all the time. I just read about a rooster killing a woman."

I watched her for a while, trying to figure her out. How much thought had she put into this? Those movie star shades hid her eyes, and I couldn't get a read on her, so I said, "You have to admit, it'd be a unique way to go. You'd definitely make the news."

I watched her struggle to suppress her smile, but her dimples gave her away. She shook her head. "Are you always so positive?"

"You know I'm not," I said, "I believe you've seen me at my worst."

Her head spun toward me, her smile gone. "Oliver? You can't be serious? Are you telling me the Oliver from last night is your worst?"

Her look and tone made me nervous to answer. The way she said it was like an accusation. Like my pain and anger weren't enough. "Is my worst not good enough for you?" I said.

Her eyes went back to the road, and she shook her head. "No, no, not at all. I just . . . I don't. . . I guess my worst looked a lot different from yours," she said, almost sounding bashful.

"You've made the whole thing a lot more bearable, Willa."

"If I had met you right after Evan and I first split, I . . . I don't think . . . It wouldn't have been a good thing. You're handling all of this a lot better than I did."

"Our situations aren't the same."

"And you're a better person than I am," she said like it was a fact.

"I'm weak," I admit. "I ran away, and she didn't even know to cancel the wedding."

"She didn't want to let you go. I can't blame her."

"Did you ever cheat on your husband?" I blurt.

"No," she said right away. "But . . . I wasn't always emotionally available to him." She swung a left, and I started laughing when I realized where she was taking us.

She parked beside the ice-cream shop. "What?" she said with a smile. "Where did you think I was taking us? I'm still in my bathing suit and cover up."

We exited the car, and as she rounded the back, I wrapped my arm around her shoulder. "Addison would never consider ice cream a meal."

Her arm went around my back. "I think they have food here too."

"Yes, fried food," I said, practically salivating.

"Have you been depriving yourself of fried food and ice cream?"

"Addison is a bit of a health nut."

"And because she's a health nut, you can't have the food you want?"

"Last year she went vegan, and I've tried to support her decision. She doesn't allow junk food in the house, and when we eat together, I try to be sensitive to her diet, so I'm not going to eat a greasy cheeseburger in front of her."

Her hand patted my abdomen, and she said, "So you have Addison to thank for your six-pack."

I smirked as her hand lingered on my abs. I arched an eyebrow as she bit her lip. Then she caught my look and dropped her hand.

"Addison has nothing to do with it," I clarified, "I work out every day."

She groaned, "Are you a gym junkie?"

"You have something against gym junkies?"

"Evan met Estelle at the gym. I'm a little bias."

"Oh, the mistress has a name. Estelle. Is she ninety?"

"Nope, she's twenty-five and gorgeous."

Anger sparks through me, and I stop, spinning her toward me. "Willa, you are gorgeous. I don't know what this ninety-year-old, Estella looks like, but I know Evan is a damn moron for letting you go. And he's an asshole for making you doubt yourself."

"You don't have to say those things, Oliver. I'm okay. Evan did me a favor by sleeping with Estelle. It hurt. It still hurts, but I was never going to be enough for him."

I lifted her sunglasses so I could see her face. "You are enough, though. You know that, right?"

She stared at me, her intense brown eyes glistening. "I don't need you to affirm my value, Oliver. I may seem defeated and bitter, but I am a strong woman, and I know my self-worth."

I nodded, accepting her answer, before grabbing her hand and pulling her toward the door. As we approached the counter, I said, "For what it's worth, I'm not a gym rat. I work out at home."

Her lips curled into a pleased smile as she stared up at the menu.

WILLA

*O*ur ice cream was melting from the heat of the day as we sat at a picnic table behind the ice cream shop. Oliver ordered a banana split. It was turning into soup, but at least he had a spoon, and his dignity remained intact while my hands were sticky with the chocolate that was dripping from my overstuffed ice-cream cone.

Oliver laughed at me as I licked furiously at my ice-cream.

We were playing twenty questions, and it was his turn. He asked, "Have you ever been sky-diving?"

"Once. When I was in college. I didn't enjoy it. It made me feel queasy, and I was too paranoid the parachute wouldn't open. Have you?"

"No, but I think it'd be fun. Did you play any sports?"

"I tried a few different sports when I was young, but I wasn't coordinated or disciplined, so nothing stuck. You?"

"I played football and baseball through high school, but I wasn't good enough to go any further. During college, I learned to surf. I really liked it, but we moved away from the ocean, and so I gave up surfing and took up swimming instead."

"Do you want to move back to the beach?" I said before licking the dripping ice-cream off my hand.

Oliver looked thoughtful. "I don't know. I don't know if I'd be any good at surfing anymore. I miss the water, but I think I would enjoy a lake or river just as much as the ocean. What about you? If you could move anywhere, where would you go?"

"Wherever my people are."

"Okay, but if you could bring those people with you anywhere, where would it be?"

"Umm, I have no idea. Maybe Hawaii if everything wasn't so expensive. I want their weather and scenery, but I want the convenience that you can't find on an island. Also, I think I'd miss the seasons. So, I really don't know."

He smiled, asking, "If you could have any superpower, what would you choose?"

"Super-speed."

"Wow, you didn't even have to think about it."

"I've already thought it through, but before I explain myself, what would you choose?"

"I'd want to fly."

I shook my head. "I knew you were going to say that."

"What's wrong with flying?"

"Nothing, except you wouldn't really be able to do it anywhere. It's pretty conspicuous. With super-speed, I would be too fast for people to track. I'd get so much done. I'd be able to travel anywhere. I'd have crazy metabolism and eat whatever I wanted. I'd be able to stop bullets, save lives, or shoplift whatever I wanted." I licked the ice cream dripping down my wrist.

"You know it's hard to take you seriously when you're licking your arm."

"I'm just trying to make you feel better about your terrible superpower choice. At least you chose your dessert wisely." I smiled, lifting the cone to see where it was dripping.

"I think it's leaking from the bottom."

I rolled my eyes. "Awesome." I moved the napkins I had wrapped around the waffle cone, and sure enough, a steady drip was coming from the bottom. I held it out, leaning forward, letting the chocolate drip on the ground as I bent over to bite into the cone.

The table shook, and I looked up to find Oliver's body shaking from his silent laughter.

I shrugged. "I never said I was dignified."

"Oh, I knew that as soon as I saw your "Wannabe" dance routine. It's refreshing."

I snickered, "You mean Addison wouldn't do this?" I bit into the waffle cone smearing ice cream on my face. "Judge me all you want," I said with a full mouth. "It's too good to waste."

I swallowed, wiping my mouth with the back of my free hand. I needed a shower at that point, anyway. "At least you know I'm not trying to impress you."

"Do you want some of my napkins?"

"That's like offering a Band-Aid to an amputee. It's beyond napkins. Do you want a bite?" I offered, moving it toward him.

"Whoa!" He slid back, out of my reach, taking his banana split with him. "I've got my own messy treat."

"I'll show you messy," I threatened, getting out of my seat to round the table. He stood, backing away as I came forward.

"There's no need for hostility," he said, laughing.

"Just one bite," I said, licking my arm as seductively as I could manage.

It seemed to work because his smile dimmed, and he stopped retreating. He set his treat on the empty table behind him and reached out for my cone. He moved it toward his mouth, but instead of taking a bite, he licked from my wrist up to my elbow, spreading goosebumps despite the heat.

His blue eyes lifted to mine and with a sexy grin, he said, "Sweet and salty."

His voice and those words made me clench my thighs together, and I made a mental note not to bite my lip. He was still grinning, knowing exactly what he was doing to me. I dropped the remainder of my cone, and I placed my sticky palm against the stubble of his jaw, smiling as I smeared chocolate ice-cream down his face.

His eyes went round, and his mouth parted with shock. I moved into him until he was leaning against the table behind him. I reached around him to dip my finger into his banana split. I lifted it, pressing it against his parted lips. He took my finger in his mouth and grabbed my wrist so I couldn't pull away. He took his time, and I stood there, wanting to jump him, even as he released my finger.

"Willa . . ." His voice was enticing.

My eyes locked on his lips, so I didn't see his hand go

behind his back, but I watched helplessly as he lifted it to smear a clump of melted ice-cream and pineapple chunks across my face.

I gasped, and he laughed.

Snapping out of my shock, I said, "Oh, it's on!" I spun around to grab the blue raspberry slushy from our table, but before I could grab it, I felt liquid—sticky and cold—dripping down my scalp to my back. I squealed, arching my spine as it descended, slithering all the way down between my butt cheeks.

I twisted, throwing my entire blue slushy at him.

"Hey!" He jumped back, but the blue drink hit him in the chest, instantly soaking through his t-shirt.

I laughed at the look on his face as he peered down at himself. He lifted his head slowly, before darting forward to grab the squeeze bottle of ketchup sitting in the middle of the table. He squeezed it, squirting a red stream across my white cover-up.

"That might stain!" I squealed.

"Then we better make it even." He squirted me again, making another diagonal line across my chest.

As soon as I slid out of my shock, I grabbed the mustard and took my revenge out on his stupid pink shorts.

To get away, he ducked behind a family sitting at one of the tables. The adults didn't seem amused by our behavior, but their kids looked excited by the chaos. I raced around the table, feeling like I was six years old chasing after the boy I liked on the playground.

He ran away from the scolding adults leaving a stream of ketchup aimed at me over his shoulder. I cornered him against the fence. His bottle was nearly empty, making a sputtering-farting sound as only a tiny bit of ketchup came splattering out.

I held the mustard out, threatening to destroy him when a shout came from the ice cream shop. The manager looked pissed as he stalked toward us like we were disobedient kids.

"You're making a mess, and you're attracting all the bugs!" The man yelled, red-faced.

Oliver stood up straight, sobering, while I looked back over the picnic area. The parents looked justified.

"Sir," I spoke, "Leroy," I said, spotting his name tag. "We may have gotten carried away. Do you have a hose? We'll be happy to clean it up."

"And pay for the condiments," Oliver added.

His offer made me want to laugh. Here we were acting like children, but the second we got caught, we reverted back to grownup behavior. It was absurd, and I didn't know how Oliver wasn't laughing. I had to bite my lip. This shouldn't have been funny, but we both looked ridiculous, him with his yellow streaked cloths and chunks of blue slushy dripping from him, and me with ice cream dripping between my butt cheeks and the red splatter covering my white top. The overpowering smell of ketchup made me slightly nauseous.

I pulled myself together and stepped forward, saying, "I'm a teacher, and he's a realtor. We really aren't irresponsible, just got caught up in the moment."

The guy seemed confused by our offer. "Fine, the hose is over there." He pointed to the back of the building and began walking that way. "Don't make me regret this. I will call the cops."

"There will be no need," Oliver said as we followed him.

"You guys might want to get cleaned up too," Leroy said, eyeing our stained clothes and sticky hair.

Oliver took the hose, and as soon as the manager went back inside, he turned it on me, threatening, "Say hello to my little friend."

I gasped as the blast of freezing water hit me in the stomach. "Oliver!"

He let go of the nozzle, saying, "I'm just giving you the shower you were talking about."

"It's so cold," I said, teeth chattering.

He stepped forward, offering, "Here, I'll be gentle."

He held the nozzle out and turned it on, letting me step into the blast this time. I got used to the chill as he helped me clean off.

He turned the hose on himself next, washing his face and spraying the blue and yellow stains all over his pastel clothes.

"Too bad, those shorts aren't see-through," I said.

The water only made the light pink shorts darker. It wasn't fair. My sheer white tunic clung to me, looking as if I wasn't wearing anything but the black bikini beneath.

Oliver handed me the hose, saying, "You need to get your face."

"Is it really that bad?" I asked.

He looked thoughtful for a moment before reaching forward to swipe his thumb over my lower lip. His hand lingered there, his thumb pressing against my bottom lip. His eyes were on my mouth, and his lips parted. I was tempted to shove him against the wall and have my way with him, but we had already been irresponsible enough for one afternoon.

There were so many reasons being with Oliver was a bad

idea, and the family at the table across the way was supposed to deter us from acting impulsively.

He seemed to snap out of it, pulling his hand away, while I stood there with dirty thoughts racing through my head. He took the hose from me since I didn't seem capable of functioning. He sprayed my hair, and the icy water dripped down my face snapping me out of my thoughts. His free hand wiped away the ice cream smudges, and despite the freezing water, the cold shower did little to cool me while his hands were touching me.

I hadn't felt this crazed since high school, and even then, I never felt this strongly about someone. I took the hose from him and continued to wash myself off before busying myself with hosing off the rest of the area. Eventually, Oliver took over, giving me the opportunity to ring out my bathing suit cover-up.

While he wound the hose back up, returning it to its spot on the back of the building, I sprawled out on the bench of the sun-soaked picnic table, hoping to dry off. Oliver went to pay the manager for "damages."

When he returned, sitting on the bench opposite me, I asked, "Boxers or briefs?" I'd been wondering ever since his shorts got wet, surprised I couldn't tell.

"Usually boxer briefs, but today I'm going commando."

I sat up, "Oliver, what if your shorts were see-through?"

"Then I guess you'd see my goods, and no one else would notice because they are all too busy checking you out."

"Oliver—"

"Ketchup or mustard?" he interrupted, "What's your go-to topping?"

"What do you think?"

He tilted his head, looking at me with pursed lips. "Knowing you it's probably something crazy like grape jelly on hotdogs."

"I prefer mustard on my hotdogs."

"Gross!"

"Oh, and I suppose you're a ketchup guy."

"I like both, but with hotdogs, it's got to be ketchup."

"Ketchup is gross! Even the smell makes me want to gag," I admitted.

"You're so strange."

"So sweet. Really, Oliver, you've gotta stop hitting on me."

"You're the one who wanted to talk about my underwear."

"Or lack thereof," I said waggling my eyebrows.

"You're going to make me crawl over this table if you don't stop."

I thought about encouraging him but did the responsible thing instead. "I'm going to the bathroom," I said, standing.

The restrooms were just inside the ice cream shop. They were single-stall restrooms, and I walked into the unoccupied women's. Before I could flip the lock on the door, Oliver burst in behind me.

"Oliver, what are you—"

His hands cupped my face and he kissed me, interrupting my question. His tongue was in my mouth before I could catch my breath, and it was a welcome intrusion. My hands clung to him, my fingers digging into his back. His hard body pressed into me, and I couldn't get enough. His hands gripped my ass as he pulled me against him. My hands were frantic, tugging at his shirt and running my hands up the smooth skin of his back.

His mouth broke from mine to run down my neck, his breath sending a chill through me.

"Oliver," I moaned.

He tugged at my bathing suit cover, and his hands were on my thighs, my hips, my waist, my breasts. I am pretty sure we would have had sex right there in that bathroom if someone hadn't knocked at the door.

He stopped kissing me, lowered my cover-up, and rested his head against my shoulder.

My hands dropped from him, but as he pulled away, I caught sight of the excitement tugging at his mustard stained shorts. I wasn't the only one anxious for more.

He looked at me with smoldering eyes, saying, "Ready to go back to the hotel?" His meaning clear.

I answered by grabbing his hand and dragging him out behind me, ignoring the look from the woman waiting for the bathroom. We rushed to the car, and I was giggling like a teenage girl.

9

OLIVER

We didn't have a long drive back to the hotel, and I couldn't stop touching her. I was an addict, and she was my fix. I leaned over and kissed the skin of her shoulder as she drove.

"Stop it, Oliver. You're going to make me wreck."

"Worth it," I breathed against her neck.

She pulled away. "Not worth it! Then we'll never get what we want."

Trying to behave, I rested back in my seat, my body too tightly wound to relax. The hotel came into view, and I blew out a breath, I knew I could make it—just one more block. But then the traffic light turned red.

She peered over at me apologetically, like stopping at the light was somehow her fault, and I couldn't take it. I pulled her face toward mine, cupping her dimpled cheeks between my palms and kissing her like I had just returned from war. She kissed back like she'd been waiting desperately for my return.

Her mouth was sweet, her kiss was hot, igniting me even

as I already burned with desire. Her hands were in my hair, her nails scraping intimately against my scalp, pulling my hair out of its knot.

Cars honked, and she pulled away from our kiss, saw the green light, and floored it back to the hotel. As soon as she parked, we started right back up, kissing, touching. Desperate to get a taste of one another.

When she finally pulled back, her cheeks were flushed against her bronzed skin. I loved her skin. It was exotic, dark enough to make me wonder about her heritage, but light enough to make me question if I was just making things up. It was just as much a mystery as she was.

Her expressive brown eyes stared at me, her face serious as our heavy breaths mixed in the confined space. She wore her emotions like most wore clothing, and I was thrilled when she smiled because I knew it was real. She was the realest thing I had ever tasted in my life, and I needed to kiss her again, but as I leaned forward, she grabbed her door handle and jetted out of the car. She ran for the hotel like a lunatic, and I was moonstruck, so I adjusted myself and exited, running after her.

Her cover-up billowed out behind her, her dark hair in wild waves as it air-dried. She slowed down as she entered the lobby, the responsible adult winning out over her impulsive inner child. But she had woken something carnal inside of me, and I didn't give a fuck what these strangers thought of me. I caught up to her and swooped her off her feet, carrying her over my shoulder instead of cradling her like a gentleman. She squealed when I picked her up, laughing so hard I could barely make out her cries to "Put me down!"

I would never put her down, not as long as she kept

laughing. It was contagious, the kind of noise that came from somewhere deep and pure, a place uncontaminated by the world. This bitter, jaded, beautiful woman who surprised me at every turn exposed a joy I didn't think her capable.

I carried her to the elevator, only setting her on her feet so I could witness her smile and taste her laughter for myself. We had the elevator to ourselves, and I devoured her, kissing her with my hands tangling in her hair as she cupped my ass. We were hot and wild and totally uninhibited. The doors opened, and we stumbled out, tripping over one another, so I lifted her. Her legs wrapped around my hips so I could keep kissing her all the way to our doors. I leaned her against the wall to free a hand to get my keycard, but she beat me to it by sliding hers out of her bag. I took it from her and unlocked her door. She dropped to her feet, and I held the door for her before following her in. She dropped her bag, slipped out of her cover-up, and spun to me.

I groaned, and she moved forward in only her bikini. My mouth met hers, and my hands roamed her skin.

The phone by her king-sized bed started ringing. She ignored it, so I did the same as we frantically lost control. It's like we were teenagers, trying to get in a quicky before our parents got home.

The phone stopped ringing, only to start back up again. "Willa?" I panted, asking if she needed to answer the phone.

She shook her head, and her hands lifted my shirt, stripping the damp material before her hands found the button on my shorts. They were still wet, which made them stick to me, but she was determined, and soon they fell to the floor, and I stepped out of them.

I felt her smile against my lips as her hands found my bare ass. "I like commando," she said.

Her bathing suit was the only thing left between us, and it couldn't come off fast enough.

I untied the string behind her back just as her phone started ringing again.

She paused, her body stiffening.

Feeling her reaction, I encouraged, "Go look."

The ringing stopped before she picked up her phone, but a second later it rang again.

She looked at the screen, and I watched her face lose some of its color. "Mom? What's wrong?"

Frantic words were spoken in quick succession from the other line. I couldn't quite make out the words, but I wanted to rip the phone away to protect her. It was too late. The moment had been ruined. I watched as everything Willa had let go of today piled back on her, contaminating her uninhibited joy.

Willa repeated, "What's wrong with her? Is she okay?"

More frantic words.

Tears pricked in her eyes, and she covered her mouth. "Oh my God! My poor baby."

Her mother started speaking slower, sounding less hysterical.

Willa looked up at me with so much guilt and sadness. I wanted to wrap her in a hug, but she wasn't done talking.

"She's such a brave girl. Okay." Pause. "Bella, momma loves you."

I felt like she had slapped me. How had she not told me?

"Thanks, Mom, I'll be there as soon as I can."

I suddenly remembered I was naked and turned away to

picked up my wet shorts. I slid into them and sat on the side of her bed, listening to her side of the conversation.

"Okay, but . . . Yeah." Pause. "I will . . . I'll try." Pause. "Love you, too," she said before hanging up.

She set her phone down on the nightstand and came to sit next to me. I looked at her when she didn't say anything. There were no tears, but she wore such a desolate expression, and I was reminded again that there was so much I didn't know about her. I wrapped my arm around her shoulder, offering comfort even as I second-guessed her.

"Do you have a daughter?" I asked.

After a long pause, she said, "Sort of."

That was all she said. She gave no explanation, and it was hard not to take her lack of answer personally. She knew my story, but only revealed fragments of her own. We promised to be honest, but we never promised to tell each other everything, so I only saw the part of her she wanted me to see. Essentially, we were still strangers, and now she was going to leave without giving me a chance.

"Are you leaving?" I asked because she hadn't made a move for several agonizing minutes.

She blew out a breath and looked at the floor, saying, "I used to teach kindergarten."

Rolling with the abrupt change, I said, "I bet you're amazing with little kids."

"I always wanted a big family—not crazy big, but maybe three or four kids. I always wanted siblings. Do you have any?"

"I have an older sister," I said, "There are three years between us, and she and I fought all the time growing up. We didn't start getting along until we were adults." And there I went, revealing more of myself while she held her cards so close to her chest.

She said, "I wish I had that. I mean Jodi has always been kinda like a sister, but I just feel like once my parents are gone, it'll just be me, all alone. I never want my kids to go through that alone, so I thought having three or four kids would be great. Do you want kids?"

"Yeah, they were always in the plan, you know, once Addison's job became more stable.

WILLA

Part of me hoped he said kids were the worst. I wanted him to tell me kids were disgusting brats. I contemplated running from the room, but I looked up and saw the crease between Oliver's brows. He was worried about me, and he'd been so patient. I could still get out of this. Sure, he'd made me feel things I hadn't felt in years, and he made me smile and laugh until my cheeks hurt, but technically, I didn't owe him anything. I could go back to being a bitch and scare him off. Then again, the truth might do that for me.

I checked the clock. It was almost six. The drive home would take me about eight hours. If I left now, I could make it home by two in the morning.

I stood, turning to him and saying, "You need dry clothes."

He didn't move, eventually saying, "Willa, you told your mom you were leaving."

There was a question in his statement. "And she told me not to," I said. "Why don't we go to your room? That way, you can put on dry clothes while I drink some of your excess liquid courage, and I can explain a little more about myself."

He watched me cautiously. I couldn't blame him. I'd given him nothing to work with.

"Oliver," I took his hand, tugging him up to a stand, "I'm gonna change, and then I'll meet you over there, okay?"

He nodded; his expression guarded.

To convince him, I said, "We'll drink Addison's Pink fucking Moscato and order food."

"Sounds like a plan." He broke from my grip, grabbed his shirt from the floor, and left.

As soon as he was gone, I put my face in my hands and contemplated what to do. I could leave. I could throw everything in my suitcase and take off. I could go home to Bella, but my mom told me not to. The vet had said she'd make a full recovery. My mom was probably exaggerating the whole thing. Bella ate weird things all the time. The abdominal x-ray was probably unnecessary, but my mom knows how much that dog means to me, so of course, she would spare no expense for my baby.

I uncovered my face and caught my reflection in the mirror over the dresser. My cheeks were pink from the sun— from my time with Oliver. I'd acted so impulsively today. I didn't even recognize the woman standing in front of me. My deep brown curls were a mess of tangles. My lips were bright and full, looking like they had been thoroughly kissed. I looked a little wild which made me laugh because this mess of a woman is what Oliver had seen all day. My reflection almost looked happy, but my dark eyes shimmered with sadness—the tears were always there, lurking just beneath the surface.

I was wearing nothing aside from my bikini, and I was comfortable. I hadn't been worried that my thighs were too big or that my stretch marks were showing. My bikini bottoms gave me a slight muffin top, and the scar on my abdomen was visible, yet this was the most comfortable I'd felt in my own skin in forever.

I thought about what my mom had told me. Apparently, Jodi had spilled the beans to my mom that I had met someone. My mom was excited, so even though she was desperate to tell me what was going on with Bella, she was adamant that I stay and see how things went with Oliver.

I had to admit Oliver brought out the good in me. I was dark and heavy, yet somehow, his light shined on that small part of me that remembered how to be happy.

Even now, he was waiting for me, and I didn't know why or what it was he saw in me. But I was excited about him too, so I changed out of my bathing suit and slipped into another comfy dress. This one wasn't as sexy as the one I wore the night before. The bright pink material hung above the knee with thin straps and a wrap that tied at the waist. The V-neck covered my silky lace bra but left just the right amount of cleavage. I wore the matching silky panties. I brought them on this trip because they made me feel sexy. Not because I was expecting to meet anyone, but now that I had, I thought I might get a chance to show them off.

I slipped into my sandals, threw the essentials into my purse, and went next door to Oliver's room. He had the door propped open with the bar from the safety lock, and I entered without knocking.

He had changed into a plain white T-shirt and blue cloth shorts. His feet were bare, and his dark hair was pulled back into a little man bun. With the stubble on his cheeks, he looked rugged and sexy as he opened a bottle of Pink Moscato.

He paused when he noticed me, and his perfect lips separated. "Well, aren't you overdressed," he said, "You look really nice. I'm on my last clean outfit." He held out his arms, looking down at himself.

"I think you look great," I reassured him.

He went back to opening the bottle before offering it to me. "Liquid courage?"

"Yes, please." I took the bottle from him.

"Do you want to go out?" he asked.

I shook my head. "No, not really." I took a swig from my bottle.

He waved a hand toward me, saying, "So all of this is just for me?"

"You make it sound like I'm all dressed up. This dress is casual. It's comfortable and makes me feel sexy."

He began opening another bottle. "Do you usually lounge around in dresses?"

"Sometimes," I said, moving around him. I rearranged the pillows and sat with my back against the headboard, leaving my shoes on the floor and setting my purse on the nightstand. I stretched my legs out in front of me and took another drink. When I looked up, Oliver was leaning against the dresser watching me.

I avoided his eyes. "My mom called me to let me know my dog was sick. She will be okay. My mom overreacts when it comes to Bella. Rightfully so. She knows how important Bella is to me."

"What kind of dog?"

"She's a Boxer and Blue Heeler mix."

He looked thoughtful. "Do you have a picture?"

I raised an eyebrow. "I have sixteen-thousand pictures of Bella." I dug my phone out of my purse and pulled up a picture of Bella. In the photo, she was sitting on the front porch with her head tilted to the side in confusion while her tongue hung out of her mouth. Oliver sat on the bed next to me, and I handed my phone to him.

He studied the picture. "She has a boxer build with the spots and coloring of a Blue Heeler."

"She's the best."

"So, she's kinda like your daughter?"

I nodded. "She's my baby." I took the phone when he handed it back, looking at Bella. "Probably the only kind I'll ever have."

God, I hated how passive and heavy that sentence was. I felt like it oozed from my tongue like molasses—substantial and sticky, and I wouldn't be able to get rid of the aftertaste until I said something else. I wanted to take it back, but it was too late.

Oliver slowly rested his head back against the head-board, looking at the ceiling. His throat bobbed, probably having no idea how to respond. I wondered if he was stuck with the aftertaste too.

"Sorry," I whispered.

He looked at me, saying, "I want to hear, but not if you don't want to tell."

I took a long breath. "I was twenty-three when I got married, and a year later, I started teaching kindergarten. I loved the kids and desperately wanted my own, but it made no sense to get pregnant. Evan was still finishing his masters, and once he finished school, the student loans crippled us financially. By the time I was twenty-six, our friends were starting their families, and I couldn't wait any longer to start our own.

"I was hoping we'd get pregnant right away, but then the abdominal pain began. It was inconsistent, which is why I put off going to the doctor. When I couldn't handle the pain anymore, Evan took me to the Emergency Room. They drew blood, ran tests, and then a woman came in with an ultrasound machine. Not the cute ultrasound machine where they place the paddle on a pregnant belly and you see the baby inside. This was an internal ultrasound, and it was the first time I was probed by an ultrasound wand."

I fiddled with the bottle in my hands as I spoke, my nails, peeling at the label as I continued, "At the time I was horrified, and then I was distracted by the sound of a heartbeat. It was only mine which the nurse kindly explained to me before it began. It still hurt. To see an ultrasound image and hear a heartbeat and know that instead of everything being exactly right, something was wrong.

"At first, they said my issue would resolve itself, but it didn't. I had so many follow-up appointments over the next few months, and every doctor on staff probed me." I paused when I realized how that sounded, surprising myself with a laugh. "Not like that."

Oliver kissed the side of my head. "You like a good probing, do you?"

I shoved him as he leaned in closer, but then I went on. "The doctors tried a few different treatments, but when nothing seemed to work, they decided surgery was my only option. They advised I have a fertility specialist do the operation to give me a better chance at having kids in the future."

I peeked at Oliver and saw his grimace. I took another swing of the Pink Moscato and continued on, "It took weeks to get into the specialist, and another month for the surgery. But it was either wait for the specialist or go in for emergency surgery and possibly destroy my chance to ever become pregnant. So, I waited.

"The pain was intense. I couldn't eat or sleep, and the pain medications came with awful side effects. I had to take medical leave from my job as it infected every part of my life.

"My insecurities grew because chronic pain makes you crazy. I was afraid my husband would stop loving me. I worried that I was a burden. I worried about not being able to give him children. I worried because we hadn't been intimate in months, and I hated the loss of control—the loss of intimacy. I felt like my body had turned into a weapon against me."

Oliver wrapped his arm around my shoulder and pulled me toward him until my head was against his chest. We sat in silence for a moment, but eventually, I went on, saying, "The surgery went well. There were a few tough days, but with the help of Evan and my mom, I made it through, and my ovaries were in good shape. And in the words of my doctor, I have a beautiful uterus."

"Damn straight," Oliver chimed.

I laughed, amazed that I was comfortable enough to talk to Oliver about this. He hadn't pushed me away as I'd thought. I also wasn't planning to tell him everything, but he had a way of gently encouraging me.

"I made Evan get checked to make sure everything was

healthy on his end while I began tracking everything, my cycles, my temperatures, everything I ate. I did ovulation predictor kits, and I read books on conceiving. Looking back, the pressure I put on us was insane. We only had scheduled sex, and we were both way too stressed. We were miserable. And we weren't conceiving. We weren't connecting. We were barely surviving. Everything felt hectic, but I didn't know how to stop because I could hear that clock ticking inside my head. I was getting older, and nothing was going as planned.

"Months of not conceiving rolled by and one day Jodi stopped by with the news she was expecting. She was two months along. I cried happy tears that she was going to have another baby. I hugged her and celebrated, and then I remembered myself, and the tears turned sad, but I kept the smile in place and shoved back my grief. I was happy first. I didn't want my pain foreshadowing the happy moment, but she knew I was hurting. It's the reason it took her so long to tell me. She was afraid her happy news would hurt me."

"I'm sure it did," Oliver added.

"I was in pain, but she didn't hurt me," I said, defending Jodi. I remembered it so vividly. After she left, I walked back into our quiet house and my smile melted. The pain was soul deep. I wandered around the house, trying to remember my purpose. I didn't want to feel ungrateful, but that day the house felt too quiet. Our tidy house bothered me. I wanted a mess. I wanted loud giggling kids running through the house, jumping on the furniture. I wanted crayon marks on the walls. I had prayed on my knees for that kind of chaos. I knew I needed to let myself feel whatever I felt even if the thoughts weren't pleasant. I needed to purge them from my body, so they didn't turn septic and eat me from the inside.

I took a deep breath, saying, "I didn't know what to do with myself after she left. Evan found me wandering around the kitchen. He pulled me into him and held me while I cried, and in between sobs, I explained that I was happy for Jodi."

I blinked back tears as they came. "Evan used to love me, and I loved that he cared enough to hold me and that he knew me well enough to know how badly I was hurting and how much I didn't want to feel the things I felt."

I sighed, picking off more of the wine label as I said, "I went through months of fertility medications and procedures while Evan and I tried to get pregnant on our own." I took a drink. "After a year of failing to conceive, we let the professionals take over. At our first treatment, Evan was sitting in his chair playing a game on his phone while I sat on the table with a thin paper drape covering my naked lower half. The syringe of his viable sperm sat on the counter, waiting for insertion. It all felt so clinical, and I was nervous. And at this opportune time, Evan casually said, 'I think we're doing this prematurely.'"

Oliver sucked air through his clenched teeth. He seemed to understand.

I took another drink. "I was so unprepared for his comment that it took me a moment to digest his statement. The hormones made me crazy, so I couldn't always trust my emotions, but at that moment, I felt completely alone. I didn't want to stress him out by taking him along with me to all thirty doctor's appointments I'd had in the past year. But he knew about them.

"I thought we were in it together. He thought we were jumping the gun. After all, he hadn't gotten prodded four times that week. He hadn't been taking the medication that gave him hot flashes and drastic mood swings. He hadn't felt every symptom for the last two years and wondered *Could that be a baby*, only to re-live the loss over and over again. He didn't have to remind himself daily that he would survive this.

"So, there I sat with my paper drape, suddenly feeling isolated and claustrophobic. It frustrated me that the doctor was taking so long. I felt my hope dying with every second. We had already waited in that room for twenty minutes. I just wanted to get pregnant already, and no one seemed to understand my desperation. My husband, who sat right next to me, complaining that he was hungry, didn't feel the walls closing in.

"No one else seemed to notice that tiny window of time closing for the next thirty days. But I felt it, and I knew what it meant. More waiting, more doctor's appointments, more probing, more pep talks in the mirror. I had been strong and brave, and suddenly, I couldn't breathe."

I took another drink to avoid the conversation because I was depressing myself. "I don't want to talk about this anymore."

"We don't have to," he reassured.

I took a few long drinks and leaned into him again, asking, "Are you close with your family?"

"Yeah, we're pretty close, I guess. My parents got divorced when I was twelve, but they still get along. They're both remarried, but at family gatherings, my mom and dad and their significant others all show up. I know it rarely works out that way for divorced couples, but we're lucky, I guess. What about you? Are you close to your parents?"

"Yeah. My mom is my best friend, aside from Jodi. My dad and I don't talk the way my mother and I do, but we still have a deep connection. It scares me that something will happen to them. They're in their late sixties, now."

"Did they want more children?"

"My parents got married when they were thirty-six. My mom was thirty-eight when she had me, and it was a risky pregnancy. She almost died during delivery, and right after I was born, they whisked her into emergency surgery. The hysterectomy saved her life, and she said it didn't matter that she couldn't get pregnant again because she had me."

"Your mom sounds sweet. How was she through all of your treatments?" he asked.

"She was supportive, but nobody really knew what to say or how to comfort me. And each month I didn't get pregnant, I felt like I was letting my parents down too. They won't be around forever."

For a moment, I was pulled into the past. Each month started with so much hope. I would take one negative pregnancy test after the other. I would convince myself I just took the test too soon, but the next day it was still negative, so I waited two more days because the negative result put a pretty big dent in my denial meter. Then I would lose hope one symptom at a time. My breasts didn't hurt, my cramps got worse, I'd start spotting. But I would make excuses, thinking maybe it was implantation bleeding or cramping. I would think about taking another pregnancy test, but I wouldn't. I couldn't, because I knew when I took that test it would rip at my heart to see another negative.

And then my period would start, and I would have no more hope.

Fuck hope.

I fucking hated how much I loved feeling hope because when it was gone, I couldn't breathe. But hope was an addiction, and I didn't know how to give it up.

After draining most of my bottle, I said, "One day Jodi came to me. She sat me down and told me to quit my job. I was so mad at her because I loved working with kids. But then I thought of all the days I hid in the bathroom to cry or to pull my shit together. 'You're okay,' was my mantra. I felt like if I said it enough, then eventually, I would feel okay. I realized being around kids was probably not the best for me at the time because it was a constant reminder of the one thing I couldn't have."

Oliver pulled back. "I like Jodi. It takes a best friend to have a conversation like that. If only Travis were more like Jodi."

I nodded. "I can't even imagine if Jodi and Evan were messing around behind my back. I'm so sorry, Oliver."

It was his turn to sigh. "I don't know what to do without either of them, Addie or Travis."

"Let's both move far away," I suggested.

"I'm still so angry," he said, dragging a hand down his jaw.

"I know that feeling."

"Do you know how long Evan was cheating on you before you found out?"

"Seven months."

"How do you know? Did he tell you? Addison refused to tell me, and it's been driving me crazy."

"Evan didn't have to tell me. I knew. It started small. I think they were only friends at first, but I caught him talking to her on the phone late one night. I should've been asleep, but Bella was a puppy, so I was getting up every few hours to let her out. Evan was outside, sitting on the patio in the dark. I cracked the door and listened for a moment, long enough to know they were talking about me. He wasn't bashing me or telling her he would leave me. He was simply confiding in another woman, kind of like I'm doing with you right now. In a way, it felt worse than if it was just sex.

"Maybe he tried not to fall in love with her," I said with a shrug. "It doesn't matter. I didn't want him telling her intimate details about me. I would have confronted him, but I couldn't find the strength to face him. I felt worthless. So, I clung to Bella because she wouldn't talk behind my back or share worried whispers with the other people who cared about me. Bella gave me a purpose and probably saved my life."

"Fuck," I wiped at my eyes. "I can't believe I'm telling you this. My mom doesn't even know this."

He kissed my forehead. "What about Jodi?"

"I love Jodi and her family, but she's always surrounded by kids, her own and the kids from the in-home daycare she runs. It's difficult to have a real conversation. She's still my best friend, but our lives are so different right now. And sometimes it hurts to be around her and her family.

"I went to her house one day when her extended family was visiting. They all had spouses and kids. I was the odd man out, but they welcomed me with open arms, feeding me, talking to me, including me, and even putting their brand-new baby in my arms. I watched the kids run around while the adults spoke in such a familial way.

"Jodi's mom started laughing with her grandkids, and it was the most joyful sound and . . ." I swallowed. "That joyful sound tore at that broken part of me. I wanted it. I wanted to give that kind of joy to my mother. I wanted all of it, and I felt like an imposter because it was not my life. Those happy people were not my in-laws. The baby I held in my arms was not my own. I walked a tightrope between smiles and tears that day. It all felt so good to pretend, but the reality of it left me feeling raw. All the things I wanted surrounded me, and yet I felt like an island lost at sea to wither alone." I wiped my tears.

Oliver pulled the bottle from my hand and leaned across me to set it on the nightstand. He wrapped me in his arms, hugging my entire body against his as if he was trying to absorb me into his own.

OLIVER

She reclined into me with her head on my chest and her arms around me. Her tears dotted my shirt. I didn't understand how I felt so attached to her.

I wanted to take away her pain. I also wanted to kick Evan's ass. No wonder she wasn't in the best headspace. It hurt me to hear her story. It hurt to know how discarded she felt. I wanted to show her what it meant to be loved.

Did I love her? It was way too soon for such strong emotions, but I felt a connection with her—a strong connection. It made little sense, but I couldn't separate myself from what she made me feel.

She tilted her head up toward me, her vulnerability showing in her expression. She'd opened the floodgates, and now she was second-guessing herself, wondering what I was thinking. I bent down to meet her full rosy lips with mine.

We shifted, readjusting, and then she was on top of me, straddling me. She brought her face level with mine. My palms ran up the outside of her smooth thighs, sliding beneath the fabric of her dress and coming to a rest at her hips.

She watched me, her face inches from my own.

She whispered, "I feel like I've known you forever."

I nodded my agreement.

She leaned in to kiss me, but I stopped her, saying, "What are we doing, Willa? This is all happening too fast. It's a bad idea."

"You're right," she agreed in a small voice.

"I don't want to hurt you," I said, cupping her cheek.

She moved to sit next to me, facing me with her legs crossed.

"We need a distraction," she said. "Let's order some food."

I thought for a moment, offering, "Or, we could go to the beach?"

"What beach?"

"Lake Michigan is only an hour away. We can get dinner and sit on the beach."

"Yes!" She sprung up from the bed, grabbing her purse and slipping into her shoes before pausing and spinning to me. "Oliver, I can't drive. I drank almost that whole bottle."

"It's okay. I'll drive. I barely had any."

She smiled, bright and perfect, and I said, "I'm not really dressed to go out."

She took me in and said, "You look super casual, and I dig it."

"Addison would make me change, and if I had nothing to change into, she'd go buy me an outfit before we went out."

"Are you asking me to buy you an outfit?" she asked with

a laugh. "Oh, fun! Please tell me you want me to pick out an outfit for you!"

"Your excitement is making me leery. I was more saying that as a thank you for accepting me the way I am."

"I changed my mind. I don't accept you. You look like a scrub, and I don't want no scrubs."

"Calm down TLC. If you buy something for me now, we won't get to the beach until dark, and no one will see what I'm wearing, anyway."

She huffed, "Fine. I'll just put up with you the way you are."

I grabbed my things, and we headed out the door.

"That wine hit me a lot harder than last night," she said as we boarded the elevator.

"What have you had today besides your ice cream?"

She thought for a moment. "I had coffee this morning."

"I think you solved the mystery."

"I am really hungry," she said.

"Do you want to stop on the way and pick something up?"

"I want a cheeseburger!" she half-shouted, as we exited the elevator.

I laughed, partly at her, but mostly at the expressions of the people waiting in the lobby. "We'll stop on the way then."

"Fast food?" she asked.

"Is that okay?"

She spun toward me, walking backward through the lobby, covering her mouth as she gasped. "What would Addison think if she could see you now?"

I shrugged. "Not my problem." I reached out and shifted her, so she didn't run into the door frame.

She giggled and spun, lacing her fingers through mine as if she had done it a thousand times before. I guided her to my truck, and the doors unlocked as we approached. I opened her door for her and waited until she climbed into the cab.

Once I came around, she was already buckled in and had the glove compartment open.

I got in, observing her as she flipped through my things. "What are you doing?"

She peeked at me, saying, "Making sure we aren't stealing someone else's car."

"What?"

"This is a really fancy truck. I'm gonna be honest. I didn't know they made trucks this fancy."

"I got a deal on it, but vehicles are pretty nice these days. You would know that if you would upgrade."

"Don't turn into a car commercial. I'll look for one, eventually."

She shut the glove compartment as I backed out of the spot, but as I drove out of the parking lot, she opened the center console. She pulled out my phone, saying, "Is it dead or off?"

"Dead. Addison killed it with all her calls and messages."

She put it back, closed the console, and leaned against it, asking, "So where are we stopping?"

"There is a row of fast-food places up here, so you can have your pick." She looked contemplative, and while she was thinking, I asked, "Would you want to go to a winery tomorrow? It's not far from here."

"Yes! That sounds like fun."

"How about this? Tomorrow, you can pick out an outfit for me to wear to the winery."

"You'll wear it no matter what?"

I narrowed my eyes. "As long as it covers everything it's supposed to."

"I promise to respect your modesty," she said with a smirk. "I know how straitlaced you pretend to be."

"Pretend?"

"Okay, maybe you're not pretending. Maybe you've just been conditioned. The clothes, the food, the way you're driving right now!" She gestured to the dashboard. "Damn, Grandpa?"

"What? Because I'm going the speed limit. I follow the rules. It's not my fault everyone else is speeding."

She barked a laugh. "Oliver you and I got into a public food fight earlier, but you won't drive five miles an hour over the speed limit."

"Those are completely different things."

"Okay, Gramps."

I grinned. "You will not peer-pressure me into speeding. Now, tell me where you want to get a burger before we pass everything."

I PULLED OUT OF THE DRIVE-THRU, AND WILLA ALREADY had straws in our drinks. She sorted through the bag, handing me my burger, but not before she folded the wrapper down so I could hold it without making a mess.

Her quirks made me happy. The fact that she was a pro at folding down fast-food wrappers made me smile. The napkins she tucked into her dress like a makeshift bib made me laugh. I was thrilled she had so easily agreed to go to the beach even though the sun was setting, and we would barely see the beach before the sun disappeared. Then she took a bite of her cheeseburger and moaned her approval, and I found I loved that best of all.

"I'm a bad influence on you," she said between bites.

"You're definitely a bad influence. Good thing I don't fall for peer pressure."

"Everyone who has peers falls for peer pressure."

"Liar!" I laughed.

"I'm serious," she exclaimed, "It's true!"

"What makes you think that?"

"It's how we fit in. It's how we feel normal—by doing the things normal people do."

"So, I have no choice in the matter?"

"It's how society works. We all fall for it to some degree because it's what we know, so without even realizing it, we fall for peer pressure."

"What if we stopped caring if we were weirdos who didn't fit in. Would that negate the problem?" I asked, peeking at her in time to see her eyes narrow.

She took a drink of her soda and said, "If we really didn't care what other people thought we would probably be criminals and we wouldn't be driving the speed limit because we'd do whatever we felt like. It'd be chaos."

"Are you saying peer pressure is a good thing?" I asked, wondering where she was going.

"I don't know. To be honest, I've never really thought about it before. I just wanted to trick you into thinking I had profound thoughts, so you didn't notice me scarfing down this cheeseburger. You were too busy thinking to realize I'm a messy eater."

I laughed, "Your bib already gave that away." Her makeshift bib was splattered with condiments, and she had mustard on her lip. I'd never been more attracted to anyone in my life. Addison and I never laughed this way. I'd never realized what I was missing, but now that I experienced it, I didn't want to give it up.

"We never finished our twenty questions," she said, "We both have two questions left."

"Go for it," I said.

She thought for a moment. "What is your favorite flower?"

I gave her a look, confused before saying, "The fire flower from Mario that lets you shoot fireballs."

She snorted, covering her mouth. "Oh my God!" she exclaimed through her laughter. "Why didn't I think of that?"

"What's yours?" I asked.

"Well, before you brought up Mario, I was going to say lilies, but now that I remember there is a flower that lets you shoot fireballs, I might have a new favorite."

"Get your own flower," I teased.

"Your superpower might suck, but at least your flower choice is spot on."

"Are you still on that? Flying would be awesome!"

"Until you got sucked through an airplane turbine," she snickered. "It's your question."

"Fine." I wanted the rest of her story but didn't want her to be sad, so I skirted the subject. "Did you and Evan ever go to marriage counseling?"

"A couple of times," she answered.

"Was it helpful?"

"That's two questions."

I was going to drop it, but then she said, "That just means I get to ask you another question."

"Fair is fair," I said.

"In general," she started, "I've always been against telling strangers my problems, present company excluded. But we were years into our fertility struggle and drowning in our situation. So, we invited a counselor in, and she was able to see options that we couldn't see because we were too close.

"In my mind, it was like Evan and I were trapped in the center of a hedge maze. We tried all the options in front of us, so in our desperation, we began chopping at the walls, trying to break free. But the hedges kept growing as we cut them down. We were wearing ourselves down and beating ourselves up, and yet, we weren't getting anywhere. We were destroying ourselves inside this labyrinth of our own making until our counselor gave us a metaphorical ladder so we could climb to the top of the hedges and see which direction to go.

"She suggested joining an online support group. I was skeptical that infertility groups existed but was shocked at the number of people struggling. She also encouraged us to do IVF, where they take the woman's egg and a man's sperm, mix them together, and after they combined, put them in a uterus.

"We had a consult with the doctor, and he felt confident it would take on the first try. We went through classes, meetings, and mounds of paperwork. I had to give myself a ton of injections, and I went for blood draws and ultrasounds every few days, but I didn't mind because I was so hopeful.

"Evan was there with me the day they retrieved my eggs. He held my hand, and we watched the monitor as the doctor drained the follicles, and the lab tech counted the number. From everything I'd read, I was expecting eight to fifteen. The tech had only counted six. I was upset but tried to rein in my reaction because at least I had six.

"I always thought I was healthy and young, so the amount and quality of my eggs would be on the higher end. I kept thinking I wouldn't lose as many as those other women who had more severe cases. I was still trying to deny my medical issue.

"The nurse delicately explained that the immature eggs would not become embryos. I knew this but wanted an immediate number. Would that leave us with five, three, two? And even if we had several embryos, that didn't mean they would make it to day-five embryos." She paused, contemplative. "I know I'm probably speaking gibberish to you right now. I'll give you the condensed version."

"It's okay. I can follow most of it. I want to know, Willa," I said so she wouldn't second guess herself.

She nodded and took a breath. "You're like my very own sexy judgmental therapist."

I scowled at her, outraged. "Judgmental?"

"And sexy," she said. "Okay, you're not judgmental, I just need you to be less . . . you."

"Oh, so, less perfect?" I joked.

"Exactly," she said, trying to stay light.

"Go on, tell me all of your problems."

She wiggled in her seat, removing her "bib," and saying,

"Evan and I went home after the egg retrieval. I took a nap, and when I woke, my cramping from the procedure had passed, but my mind was a train wreck. Evan had to run out, and I was so relieved he wasn't around because then I didn't have to try to hide what I was feeling. And honestly, I couldn't understand what I was feeling.

"I was stunned by how little control I had over the situation. It was all up to the lab. The helplessness I felt was overwhelming. Evan had his own emotions, but I was too raw to focus on him.

"The lab called two days later to tell me we had four embryos. I could handle four. I was expecting at least a couple of the eggs weren't mature enough. The embryologist informed me they would call with another update in two days. That was forty-eight hours away. It was 2,880 minutes until the next call, and I didn't know what to do for the next 2,880 minutes?

"I never expected to feel so helpless during the process. It was hard to leave something so fragile and important— something that should be happening inside of my body—in the hands of a stranger. With the other treatments, I could at least fake the element of control, but with this, it was entirely out of my hands. All I could do was find distractions until the next phone call."

She gasped, "Oliver, pull over! Pull over! There's a thrift store."

She said this as we were already passing the parking lot, then looked disappointed we didn't make it. As I pulled into the next lot to turn around, I asked, "You want to go thrifting instead of going to the beach?"

"I want both!" She slapped my arm excitedly. "I have

such a great idea! The hotel has washers and dryers, right?"

"I think so. If not, they have a laundry service," he said.

She pulled out her phone and began searching while I pulled into the thrift store parking lot.

"They do," she said. "It's next to the gym. We have to use quarters. Or we can use their laundry service."

"Willa, what are you thinking? You're being very intense."

She unbuckled and turned her whole body toward me. "Okay, here's what I propose. We find outfits for the winery. I will find an outfit for you, and you find something for me, but neither of us sees what we pick for each other until we are getting ready tomorrow."

"You trust me that much?"

"We still have the same modesty rule, and remember, we will have to be seen with each other so keep that in mind."

"This could be really fun. I'm in, but I have one more rule. It has to be weather appropriate. I don't want to pass out because you put me in a winter coat in the middle of the summer."

"You think your problem will be too many clothes?" She laughed, and I didn't know how concerned I should be, but I didn't know the people here, so I guess it didn't matter . . . much.

"Okay, I'm in," I said.

She held out her hand to shake, and I took it. "Okay, break!" she said before darting out of the truck. She turned toward me as we walked inside, saying, "No peeking! And be quick. I don't want to miss the sunset."

I nodded and started for the women's section while she went to the men's.

12

WILLA

Oliver wore a mischievous grin as we walked out of the thrift store carrying our bags. We'd had to exchange clothing sizes before we really started our search, but we were quick about it, making it in and out in fifteen minutes. I had been true to my word and hadn't peeked at his purchase, but I was so curious.

We climbed into his truck, stashing our bags in separate places. He started the vehicle, and as we got back on the road, he said, "You stopped in the middle of your story earlier."

It surprised me that he wanted me to continue my depressing story, but I started up where I left off. "People say all you need is one, and though it's a nice thought, each embryo transfer has a thirty to fifty percent chance of becoming a baby. That—at best—is the flip of a coin! So only needing one was not the comfort people meant it to be.

"Two days passed, and I got the call from the embryologist. I expected we might lose one or maybe even two, but this news seemed much worse. The guy rattled off some numbers, and I wasn't quite sure what he meant, but it didn't sound good. Then I had to wait another 2,880 minutes.

"We never expected that we might lose them all. We spent every penny we had and couldn't afford to go through another round.

"I wondered how I could have been so stupid that I hadn't even considered the option of having no embryos to transfer. I always pictured we'd have like eight or maybe nine. It wasn't a matter of if it would work; it was a matter of when it worked. I was so unprepared because hope had lifted me so high only to let me fall. Some days I feel like I'm still falling."

"I'm so sorry, Willa," Oliver whispered, "Life can be so painful."

His words fueled me to continue, "I fucking jumped in with both feet and all my hope, and potential joy was ripped out of my heart via a phone call. They called on my way into work. I was so frantic that I accidentally sent them to voice-mail, and I'm so glad I did. It was a mercy because I didn't want to talk to the lab tech after they gave me devastating news. They basically said the embryos were incomplete and missing parts of their structure. The quality was so poor that they had already discarded them. All of our little em-babies were gone.

"I listened to this message less than five minutes before I had to be at work. I called Evan, but he was in meetings all morning. I needed to talk to someone, so I called my mom as I pulled into the school parking lot. When she answered, I couldn't speak. I didn't want to say the words out loud. I didn't want it to be real. I made a poor attempt to speak as a sob ripped my chest in two. My mom cried with me, trying to soothe my broken heart as hers broke too. I talked to her for a few minutes before I walked into work. I was an absolute mess. I pulled myself together and got through the day by compartmentalizing.

"After that, the grief came in waves. My emotions were all over the place. I was angry we spent all of our savings and devastated it didn't work. One moment I was desperate to try again, and in the next moment, I wanted to use our money on things that wouldn't break our hearts and leave us with nothing but sore bodies and empty pockets.

"I had a hard time accepting the loss, maybe because I had never failed so hard at something before. I put all my eggs in that basket, only for them to be deemed defective and discarded. I felt like a piece of me died along with our em-babies.

"There were options. The first avenue I explored was the one that wouldn't break my heart but living a life without children felt like a broken life for me. Adopting was just as expensive and potentially even more heartbreaking. So, we waited six months, took out a loan, and tried again.

"I didn't think I could go through it again. I swear I had PTSD. Every time I stepped into that doctor's office, I would sweat, and my heart would race. Every doctor's visit reopened my past trauma. It was more emotional the second time. We went into debt for something we weren't sure would even work. Emotionally I was a train wreck, but medically, the process was the same. Only the second time, we ended up with two transferable embryos.

"I was over the moon happy. I'd waited so long. We transferred both embryos, and a few weeks later, I found out one stuck. It was my first positive pregnancy test. I wanted to frame it, but that's gross and weird.

"I will never forget hearing my baby's heartbeat and seeing the flutter on the ultrasound screen. I got to experience morning sickness, and I've never been more grateful for something so awful. Then, eight and a half weeks in, I started bleeding. My OB told me to go straight to the hospital, and they took me back right away. I was . . ." My words drifted, and for a second, I was back there.

I was in that hospital room, lying in bed, staring at the blank TV screen.

There in that hospital room, I found out what it was like to lose a piece of my soul. My heart kept beating despite the gaping hole through the center, and I was breathing, yet I knew I would never catch my breath again.

Then I realized that someone in that hospital was probably giving birth to a healthy baby even though they didn't deserve it—even though they did nothing but have a quick fuck to make such a precious gift—even though there was no way they could love their baby as much as I loved the little peanut that I had to flush down the toilet.

"Willa?" Oliver's voice snapped me out of my memory.

I was crying. Not a single tear that gracefully leaks from one eye like you see on TV. These tears were dripping from my chin and running down my neck. They slid along my chest, falling between my breasts where the moisture caught in the lining of my bra, right over my beating but broken heart. Right where the grief belonged.

I forgot to breathe for a moment and gasped as I wiped my tears. "Sorry, Oliver."

"Never apologize for feeling sad."

I swallowed and grabbed napkins from the glove compartment. As I mopped up my face, I said, "We lost our baby, and I hated that I was surrounded by people who didn't have any idea what I was going through. I wanted everyone to hurt the way I hurt, and yet I didn't. I just wanted people to understand and give me the space I needed to grieve like I had lost a baby. But most people didn't see it that way, so I shoved the grief down as far as it would go until it ripped me apart from the inside, turning me into nothing more than a walking massacre living beneath a flimsy smile."

"God, Willa, that's awful."

It was awful, and there had been triggers everywhere. They were unavoidable. I held it together the best I could, but there were still times I would be in the middle of something and out of nowhere an all-consuming sadness pulled the breath from my lungs and the tears from my eyes.

I said, "We didn't want people to feel sorry for us. We wanted them to care, but we wanted peace, without the words of friends and strangers poking at our hearts in the most unpleasant way."

I stopped talking after that. It was a bad idea to bring this up. I didn't want to relive the worst part of my life. I didn't want to look too closely at all the places where I fell short.

Oliver didn't deserve this negativity, so I reminded him that there was some good. "Life tastes bitter sometimes, but I have drops of sweetness, like my mom and dad, Jodi, Bella. I don't take them for granted, at least I try not to."

"What about me?" he asked, "Am I a sweetness?"

"Like honey," I said.

There was a long span of quiet, and I felt anxious. I had just opened up to him, telling him so much about myself—

more than I'd ever told anyone, and he was so quiet. I wanted to know what he was thinking. Did I just change his opinion of me? What if he regretted asking me to go to the beach?

"Fireworks or sparklers?" Oliver asked, out of nowhere. It was such an abrupt change of topic. I looked at him and he was grinning.

When I didn't answer right away, he said, "I like sparklers more than fireworks. Most people judge me for my choice, but sparklers remind me of my childhood, and I still like to spell things out with my sparklers."

Leave it to Oliver to make me smile.

"I like both," I said, "but while sparklers are fun, they don't give me that vibration in my chest that I get from the fireworks. Nothing against sparklers, but I like fireworks more."

Oliver looked out his side window, saying, "The sun is going down. I don't know if we will make it in time."

"How far are we?"

"It's just up here but look." He pointed to his left, and I saw a glimpse of water.

"So, I have a bonus question to ask you," I reminded him.

"Go for it."

I watched him carefully, asking, "What's your favorite sex position?"

His head jerked to me, and his eyes caught on my smile. His eyes traveled down my body before they flicked back to the road. "Wouldn't you like to know," he said with a chuckle.

I asked so I could see him squirm, but damn did it backfire.

♥ ♥ ♥

WE PARKED ON THE SIDE OF THE ROAD NEXT TO A SAND dune that separated us from the lake. The signs posted said this stretch of beach was part of the state park. He led me down a sandy path between dunes. I heard the water lapping at the shore before I saw it, and then we were there.

We stood on the beach, inches away from the reaching waters that swayed in and out. I inhaled the fresh air, and the cool breeze blew through my hair, cooling my skin as I looked out over the water. I knew the Great Lakes were big, but I felt like I was standing before a vast ocean. Oliver stood next to me, taking in the same breathtaking scene. The sky extended forever, its faded blue hues singed by fiery oranges and glowing yellows.

We made it just in time to watch the sun's yellow flame melt into the lapping navy waters, but even after the sun had dipped below the waves, a halo of golden light burned the sky. Like molten lava, a red glow seared across the horizon. The heavens blushed a ruby red with streaks of pinks and oranges.

We watched in silence as the colors liquified, melting together until the dark hues overtook the scorching colors. Purple and navy overwhelmed the night sky, providing a dark place for the crescent moon to shine. The waves turned black while the dark heavens gave birth to thousands of glistening stars.

Oliver turned to me with a serene look. "We made it," he whispered.

I nodded, my pulse responding to him. The dark made me more aware of how alone we were. I inhaled, filling my lungs with the fresh breeze. I closed my eyes, battling with my libido that wouldn't quit. She was making overtime wages this week. I desperately needed her to take a vacation.

Oliver's hand brushed my cheek, and my eyes flew open. He was watching me, his hand holding my cheek. His gaze was too appealing, so I avoid his eyes, but his lips caught my attention, compromising my resolve.

"I wish I could take your pain, Willa."

I swallowed. Then swallowed again. I stepped toward him, and he held my face between his hands. He leaned in, his soft lips teasing mine. His tongue was a welcomed friend, and my palms greeted his chest, wanting to push him away almost as much as I wanted to pull him closer.

Pleasant heat filled my body, and his hands dropped from my face to run down my sides. Even as he held me, I couldn't stop sinking. I was falling in love with him. And I needed to pull away to protect my heart. But my heart wanted him, and it so rarely got what it wanted. So I wrapped my arms around his neck and clung to him, abandoning the logic that told me this was temporary, that this would never work. The logic that said we had separate lives filled with so much drama that we felt the need to run away. We were escaping together, but we lived in different states. Our lives were so dissimilar, and the thing we had most in common was heartbreak.

We were a disaster, but the chemistry was real. I tried to stay in the moment with him, wanting to explore the pleasure he promised, but I had opened up about my past, and now it loomed like a shadow, darkening my thoughts and tainting our passion.

I pulled away before the tears started. He let me go, and

I turned my back to him, taking a few steps away into the wet sand along the shore. I slipped out of my sandals and bent down to pick them up.

I was ashamed I wasn't strong enough to be in the moment with him. I was ashamed I couldn't get control over my emotions. I wiped a tear, wishing I could take back all the words I'd spoken to him today. I wanted him to think I was strong.

"Willa?" he said, walking up behind me.

I took another step closer to the lake, feeling the icy water wash over my feet. Summer had just started, and the lake had not had time to adjust to the warmer temperatures. I forced myself into the frigid water until the waves lapped just under my knees. Oliver wouldn't follow me out here. He had too much sense.

Chills spread up my legs, and goosebumps raised on my arms. I held in the shiver and did my best to make it look like I was comfortable, not crazy. Maybe he would think this was just one of my many eccentricities—like I couldn't get enough of the view until I became part of it.

"Willa, it's fucking freezing," Oliver hissed, attempting to wade into the water. "Did you go out there just to get away from me?"

I guess I hadn't fooled him, but I didn't want to tell him what I was doing, so I stayed quiet, looking out over the dark waters, trying not to think about what was swimming around my feet.

"Fine." He sounded disappointed. "I'll give you some time."

I looked over my shoulder, watching as he walked away. My legs acclimated to the cold as I stood there wondering how to calm myself down. Wrapping my arms around myself, I was tempted to sink deeper. What would Oliver think if I just disappeared into the waves? He'd probably call a search team out here.

I was afraid to face him, overwhelmed by my fear, but what was I so afraid of? Perhaps, it was a delayed response to me opening up old festering wounds.

I had let him in which was terrifying, but more frightening still, was he didn't run away. He seemed to accept me, and it filled me with warm feelings and hope.

Hope and I had a contentious relationship, and I was already terrified of my own emotions. I'd given him the power to hurt me, but maybe if we weren't intimate, I could convince myself that I hadn't let him in. I wasn't sure I had the strength to care about him the way I did.

I wasn't ready for Oliver, and I doubted he was ready for me. I was too intense, and he was too perfect. His biggest flaw with Addison was self-sacrifice. She might have muted his joy, but I would crush him with my neediness.

13

Eventually, she came back to dry land. I stood down the beach, waiting for her with a blanket folded over my arms. I had retrieved it from the truck while she was having her moment.

"All better?" I asked as she approached.

She stared at me, looking so sad. "I'm sorry, Oliver. I overreacted but getting involved is a bad idea. You even said so yourself."

"I didn't mean to push you," I said, then offered, "Come with me."

I led her toward the truck but veered to the right, climbing a sandy incline that took us to the top of a sand dune. It overlooked the lake, and the moon reflecting off its crystal surface. I unfolded the blanket, laid it out, and without saying anything, I sat down and waited for her to sit next to me. She sat with hesitation.

"I didn't bring you up here so I could make a move," I clarified. "I just thought it was a nice spot, and I'm not ready to go back yet."

She looked at me, her knees were bent in front of her, and she wrapped her arms around them, saying, "Name one thing you don't like about yourself."

"Why?"

"Just do it," she said, looking back out at the waves.

I thought for a moment before offering, "I'm too passive."

"I think people call that easy-going."

"Yeah, but I give in too quickly. Like your question, for example. I didn't want to answer, but I did."

"Does that mean I'm too pushy? I made you tell me."

"It's different with you."

"How so?" she asked.

The breeze blew her hair from her shoulder, and she shivered.

"Stay here," I said, standing. "I'll be right back."

"That's what they say in scary movies right before they die," she said, sounding serious as she looked up at me.

I laughed and bent, kissing the top of her head. "I'll try not to die."

I went to the truck to grab the jacket I had in the back seat. She was sitting in the same position, looking out over the water when I returned. She didn't even look over as I draped the jacket over her shoulders and sat next to her.

She grabbed onto the jacket, holding it around her as she said, "What makes me different?"

"What?"

"You said it's different with me. Why?"

I crossed my legs and said, "You push me to look at myself when I'd rather not. You force me out of my comfort zone and make me face things that I'd rather not examine too closely. You're the reason I learned that Addison controlled my life. I've been willingly letting someone make all of my decisions for eleven years." I uncrossed my legs, ready to jump to my feet, feeling unbelievably angry. "Eleven years and she was fucking Travis."

Willa offered me a rock. I took it and looked at her in question.

"You looked like you needed to throw something," she supplied.

I stood and threw the rock into the waves. It wasn't enough. I needed something bigger. I needed something I could break. "Do you have any more dishes?"

"Sorry, I'm fresh out," she said, handing me a larger rock.

"Where are these coming from?"

"There is pile over here. Someone must have left them just for us." She stood next to me, her own rock in hand. Her whole body seemed to wind up before she released the rock, shouting, "Fuck you, Evan Durban!"

I followed her lead, shouting to let the rage out. I was mad at Addison and Travis, but mostly I was mad at myself, and I couldn't yell, "Fuck me!" That would not come off right, so I shouted without words as I chucked rock after rock into the lake.

Willa shouted with words. Every single rock had a purpose. "Fuck you, Estelle! Fuck you, ovaries! Fuck you, life! Fuck you, God!"

She gasped for air after shouting the last one, and I realized she was bawling. She stopped picking up rocks, and her body shook as she shouted at the night with tears pouring down her face.

I stared at her in the midst of her anger and pain. She intimidated me. She was like a wild cat, elusive and dangerous, but I wasn't afraid of her. I was frightened of my reaction to her. When a lion roars, you run the other way, but I wrapped this lioness in my arms, holding her until her breaths slowed and her tears stopped.

"Do you want to go?" I asked into her hair.

She nodded, and I released her slowly. She bent to grab the jacket that slipped off, and I gathered the blanket. Together, we walked back to the truck.

We got in, and I pulled out onto the road, reaching for the radio, but stopped when she started speaking.

"Do you think God is punishing us?" Her voice was soft.

I shook my head, "I don't think that's how God works."

"I thought I was doing everything right, Oliver. I mean, I graduated from college before we got married. Evan and I both got good jobs and bought a house before we started trying for a family. We went to church every Sunday. We worked so hard to do everything just right, and then my body let us both down."

She shook her head as she went on, "I did everything right and created this beautiful life, but it all fell apart. Evan didn't even know if he wanted kids, but then he goes and does everything wrong. He cheats on his wife, shacks up with his girlfriend, and before our divorce was even finalized, he gets her pregnant.

"They are happy. He gets everything I ever wanted, and I am the only one left to suffer. I know life isn't fair, but does it have to be so cruel?"

I didn't know what to say because life was really fucking unfair sometimes but talking about it only made me angry at the injustice. It wasn't the time to tell her that there was always someone who was going through something worse because that would only make her feel like her feelings weren't valid.

When I didn't answer, she asked, "What if Addison got pregnant with Travis's baby?" In the same breath, she said, "I guess that's not the same. What if she was pregnant with your child and then left you?"

"That's not even a possibility." I smirked. "She doesn't want to mess up her career with an unplanned pregnancy, so even though she's on birth control, she always made me wear a condom."

"The horror!" she gasped.

"At least I didn't catch whatever Travis might have."

"What are you going to do when you go home? Where will you live?" she asked.

"I'll probably stay at a hotel until I get an apartment."

She bit her lip. "Evan basically handed me our house in the divorce. I think it made him feel better about everything, but I don't want to live there. I never loved that house, but Evan did, so I learned to love it. It's far away from the school where I teach, and the taxes are outrageous. I'm living with my parents until our house sells."

"How long has it been on the market?"

"Two weeks. My realtor is dealing with it. I told him to just go with the highest offer. I really don't want to be involved."

We were quiet for a while, and I broke the silence, saying, "Do you think Addison has called off the wedding? I mean, how does one go about notifying people?"

She shrugged, suggesting, "Post it on social media."

I laughed. "Addison would never post it. She'll try to keep it as quiet as possible."

"I'm surprised you didn't want to tell your family."

"I don't want to tell anyone, especially them. I can barely wrap my head around how stupid I've been. I'm not ready to deal with other people's reactions. I can't imagine what my parents think. My sister, too. They all love Addison. She's been part of my life for so long that I feel like they'll be angry with me for calling it off."

"She cheated on you!"

"I know, but people won't understand. Addie is loveable. You could say she slept with five men and I'd still come off as the bad guy in all this. I don't even want to drag her name through the mud. I just want this to be over."

"Oliver, don't go back to her," she said, sounding desperate. "Promise me you won't. You deserve so much better. I don't care how great Addison is. I don't care if she cured cancer. I mean that'd be awesome, but it still wouldn't change what she's done to you and everything you've given up for her. You put Addison on a pedestal, doing everything to ensure her happiness. You deserve a partner. You deserve someone who loves you as much as you love them. God, Oliver, you are easy to love. You will find the right person, but it isn't Addison."

"I know. That's why I left and let my phone die. I needed time to process without the pressure from everyone around me."

She looked out the window, saying, "I used to believe we made our own fate, but I think we needed to meet each other exactly when we did. You give me hope, Oliver. You make me believe that life won't always suck. Thank you for that."

"Only you would thank me for giving you hope, in my most hopeless time. You act like I'm not a mess."

She balled up the jacket and put it against the window, using it as a pillow. As she leaned against it, she says, "One day when I was venting to Jodi, she told me that she didn't understand how I was handling things so well. I didn't feel like I was handling things well, but she went on to say every time she had a sleepless night or a rough day with her baby, she remembered me and how much I would give to be having that rough day or sleepless night, just to hold my baby in my arms. She said because of seeing me in my struggle; she appreciated her kids more. I was thankful that someone else could take something positive away from what I was going through."

"You think someone can benefit from my situation."

"I already have," she said in a small voice with her eyes closed. "Everything happens for a reason sounds cliché, but if all of this hadn't happened, then we wouldn't have met." The silence hung between us, and I wondered if she had fallen asleep, but she softly added, "And I really needed to meet you, Oliver."

"I needed to meet you too," I said just as softly. We still had a way to go, so I turned music on, keeping it low.

Her body relaxed, and her breathing evened out, long and slow, and I knew she was sleeping. She didn't wake up when I pulled up to the hotel or when I turned off the engine.

This was the second time she'd fallen asleep while she was with me, and I was envious of how relaxed she looked. Her mouth was open, and she was drooling on my jacket. It made me chuckle, and I pulled out her phone and took a picture of her.

The flash made her stir, and I dropped her phone back in

her bag and rested my hand on her shoulder. "Willa, wake up. We're here."

"Okay," she mumbled, her eyes still closed. "You go on without me. I'll sleep here."

"I'm not going to leave you out here. Come on."

"I don't wanna," she whined.

"Do I need to carry you like a kid?"

"Yes," she mumbled.

I smirked, saying, "you asked for it."

I grabbed her purse before going out my side and rounding to hers. I had every intention of throwing her over my shoulder, but when I opened the passenger door, her eyes stayed closed while her arms opened up, trusting me to scoop her into my arms.

My heart skipped and I forgot how to breathe. Her sleepy eyes cracked open, and she wore an intimate smile. There was nothing sexual about it, but it hit me in the chest, and my whole body reacted to her. I lifted her from the seat, cradling her body against mine while her arms wrapped around my neck and her face burrowed against my shoulder. I shut her door and readjust her when we neared the building to make sure her dress was covering her ass. As we entered the lobby, she whispered, "Some days, I wonder if I'll love again, but you, you make it hard not to fall in love with you."

I pretended not to hear her because I didn't know if she meant what she was saying, and I didn't know how to respond. I didn't want to fall for her. The emotions we built our friendship on were ugly, and I didn't want to associate the ugly with her. I didn't want to compare everything she did to Addison. I needed an Addison cleansing before I could ever be with Willa, and she would need something too, maybe some counseling.

It didn't mean I didn't love her. I just couldn't let myself love her the way I wanted to.

We rode the elevator up, and I stopped at her door. "I need to get the key, Willa."

She pulled it out of her bra, and her dress fell sideways giving me a peek at her pretty lacy bra. She scanned the card, the lock clicked, and I carried her to her bed, covering her with the fluffy white comforter. She moaned and cuddled up to her pillow. I kissed her forehead, whispering, "Goodnight, Willa. Wake me in the morning so we can do our laundry."

She didn't respond, so I made a mental note to check on her in the morning. I turned off her light before leaving.

I couldn't sleep. I was too wound-up. I entered my room and paced back and forth a few times before I decided to go get the bags from the car. I would have the laundry service clean them. That way, I wouldn't ruin my surprise.

I grabbed both bags from the truck and peeked in the one I bought for Willa. It's probably a good idea to have them clean hers anyway because I didn't want to ruin the feathers and sequins that hung from the short gold dress.

14

The sun gleamed through the sheer curtains. At first, I thought I must not have closed the blinds, but then I realized there were no blinds and the sun was on the wrong side. Wait, no. I was on the wrong side of the bed. No, again. I no longer had a side of the bed, and this was not my bed, anyway. I looked around the room; my mind slow to catch up. Hotel. I was at a hotel. My heart was racing all because I couldn't remember where I was.

I looked at the clock. Seven-seventeen.

The sun didn't wake me, my bladder did, and now that I knew where I was, I got out of bed and rushed to the bathroom.

My eyes were puffy, and my head hurt. The previous night came back to me, and I remembered everything I had said and done yesterday. But I didn't remember getting in bed. I remembered falling asleep in the truck and then . . .

"Damn it!" I told Oliver to carry me up to my room. He should have objected. I wasn't even drunk. I wish I were, at least that would give me an excuse for my behavior. I remember being in his arms and feeling safe and loved. It was crazy.

I wondered when we were going to the winery, and then I remembered the thrift store clothes. I looked around the room but didn't see them. I'd have to see if Oliver brought them up from the car. He probably peeked at his outfit. I hope he didn't. I couldn't wait for his reaction.

I got into my travel stash of medication, so I could try to get rid of my nagging headache. I still had sand on my legs which meant there was probably sand in my bed. That's okay, I would sleep on the other side.

I showered and slipped into a pair of lounge shorts and a t-shirt. I threw my wet hair on top of my head, slipped into flip flops, and slid the room key into my pocket before leaving my room. I thought about knocking on Oliver's door but didn't want to wake him if he was still sleeping.

I rode down on the elevator with tired strangers, but we all seemed to have the same goal. Breakfast. While they went to pile their plates, I stopped for the necessities. The hotel's coffee wasn't top of the line, but I wasn't picky.

I took a sip and almost moaned, needing the morning pick me up.

"Enjoying your roasted bean water?" Oliver's voice startled me from behind, and I spun to face him. He was trying not to laugh at me.

"Did you just call this bean water?"

"Roasted bean water. And yes, that's what it is."

"Yeah, but that makes it sound gross."

"It is gross."

"What are you drinking?" I asked, pointing to the cup in his hand.

"Green tea."

I made a face of disgust. "You're drinking hot leaf water. And you think coffee tastes bad. Green tea is the grossest tea."

"It's better for you than coffee."

"I don't care. It tastes like leaves."

"And beans are better?" he asked with a smirk.

"Leave my roasted bean water alone." I laughed. "Have you already eaten?"

"No, I got down here just before you did. I dropped our thrift store clothes off at the front desk to get cleaned. I explained to them that I was not allowed to see what was in the one bag and asked for them to wait until I left to pull it out."

"You're lying?" I accused.

"Scout's honor," he said, holding up the correct fingers.

"Were you actually a boy scout?"

"I was," he said.

"Okay, boy scout, why didn't you peek?"

"Because it's supposed to be a surprise and I wouldn't have wanted you to peek at yours."

"Fair enough," I said, grabbing a plate and going through the buffet of food.

We sat at a table on the outskirts of the lounge area, and I said, "Sorry for unloading my story on you yesterday and then crying and screaming like a lunatic."

"I think what you did yesterday was brave and cathartic. I like that you're real with me. I can't imagine you doing that with just anyone. I'm honored."

His answer made me feel better about trusting him. I took a bite of my food, feeling warm inside.

"Besides," he added, "I was screaming and telling sad stories too."

"I made you carry me to bed," I moaned, apologetically.

"You were too fucking cute. I couldn't say no to you. You're sweet when you're sleeping, even though you drooled all over my jacket."

"That sounds accurate," I said. "I would apologize, but I get scolded when I try."

He smiled, and between bites, he asked, "What time do you want to go to the winery? They have a restaurant and a live band in the afternoon. They open at ten, but I don't think the hotel will have our clothes ready until noon."

"I'm fine playing it by ear. Do you want to go swim in the meantime?"

"Didn't you just take a shower?" He reaches over to touch the hair knotted on my head.

"Yeah. I still had sand on me, and I never actually had a proper shower since our food fight. I felt gross, but I can shower again. It's no big deal."

He opens his mouth to speak, but I beat him to it. "Addison would never be okay with that."

He laughs. "That's not what I was going to say, but it's close enough."

"Are you sure everyone loves Addison? It sounds like she's got a stick up her butt."

"I don't want to talk about Addison today. Can we do that? Can we just stay in the present today? No talking about exes or what's going to happen in the future. Let's just live today to the fullest."

I smiled. "I love that idea!" I stood up, grabbing our empty plates. I dropped them off and got a refill of coffee in my to-go cup.

Oliver waited for me by the bank of elevators, and we rode up together. "I have to call my mom and see how Bella is doing. I meant to do that last night."

"Are we still going to the pool?"

"If you want," I said, stepping off the elevator.

"I'm always down for a swim."

I pulled my keycard out before we got to our rooms and Oliver said, "I'll leave my door cracked. Just come over when you're ready to go down."

"Okay, see you soon," I said, entering my room.

FUCKITY FUCK FUCK. I WASN'T THINKING CLEARLY. I wasn't thinking at all. Oliver without his shirt on was trouble, but Oliver rubbing against me while shirtless and wet was dangerous. We were trying to keep things platonic, but the problem was, we had already crossed a line, and now we were trying to uncross it. It was like putting the toothpaste back in the tube or whipped cream back in the can. It couldn't be done. At least not easily.

I already knew what his tongue felt like in my mouth and what his body felt like against my own. I'd already seen him naked. I knew what he was packing, and I really wanted to unpack it.

I hadn't flirted with anyone in years. I didn't even think I knew how, but I was flirting with disaster, and his name was Oliver.

Because it was early, we had the outdoor pool mostly to ourselves. We had already raced a few laps, and Oliver had beaten me every time except once when he let me win. We learned that my underwater handstands were better than his, but his cannonballs were bigger than mine.

Those were all hands-off activities, but now he was trying to lift my feet so I could jump from his hands. There was body contact. I craved it and judging by the way his touch lingered and strayed; I think he wanted it too. So, there we were, daredevils flirting with one another like adolescent teens.

I held his shoulders for balance as he lowered his hands underwater. I lifted my feet into his palms and balanced against him until I felt steady. Then he started lifting me out of the water.

I was almost all the way up when my foot slipped. He tried to cushion my fall, but his hand ended up between my legs with nothing but my swimsuit between my most delicate parts and his fingers.

It was an accident, but I didn't want it to be. He pulled his hand away, and his arms wrapped around me as we laughed together. My hands were on his shoulders, and as much as we tried to laugh it off, I saw the hunger in his expression and felt the stiffy in his shorts.

I wanted to shout danger or push away, but I wanted him more.

"We're living in the moment, right?" I asked.

His eyes lit up, and he nodded. I grabbed his face and kissed him. He kissed back, but I pulled away quickly, saying, "Do you want to see my room?"

"Fuck, yeah."

I smiled and pushed away from him, feeling like a tease, but kids were swimming fifteen feet away. We couldn't do any of the things I wanted there in the pool.

I climbed the ladder and ran for my things. Then turned back, wondering how Oliver would hide what was happening in his shorts. He got out of the pool, and I was slightly disappointed that his swim trunks weren't tented. I didn't bother with my cover-up. I just wrapped the towel around me, tossed Oliver his, grabbed our things, and headed for the door.

He followed, grabbing my hand on our way to the elevator. It took a minute for the doors to open. Oliver put me slightly in front of him and pulled our interlaced hands to his shorts.

I felt the bulge as he whispered in my ear. "I saw you looking. Don't worry. It's there."

I looked over my shoulder, saying, "How did you hide that?"

He grinned a cocky grin and shrugged. "Skill."

The doors opened. I tugged him forward, slammed my hand on the three, and frantically tapped at the button to close the doors. When they finally began to close, I spun to face Oliver. He was on me immediately, but not in the way I expected. Instead of kissing my mouth, he pulled my towel down, moved one of the triangles that made up my bikini top to the side, bent down and his mouth closed around my nipple.

I gasped, and my hands grabbed the back of his head while I squeezed my legs together. I wasn't going to make it. Every swipe of his tongue added heat to the fire burning inside me. It was spreading. I could feel the heat in my cheeks. Pleasure cascaded through me.

Then the elevator dinged, and Oliver stood, pulling the triangle back over just before the doors opened. I could hardly catch my breath. I was sure my face was pink, and Oliver's grin was full of mischief.

As an explanation, he said, "Your nipples have been driving me crazy for the last hour."

"So, you could see my hard nipples?" I breathed, and his smile grew. "I am so going to write a review for this suit when I get home."

He led me down the hall. And I said, "Do you think they have cameras in those elevators?"

"If they do, someone just got a show." In the next breath, he said, "Your room or mine?"

"Your room. I have sand in my bed."

He unlocked his door and threw it open, pulling me inside. I stumbled in, and the first thing I saw were the clothes hanging in the open closet by the door. The garments were covered in clear plastic bags with dry cleaning slips attached.

I gasped. "Oliver is that for me?"

He turned toward the gold dress glittering with sequins and iridescent bronzed feathers. It would be pretty if it weren't so . . . much. It was over the top, ridiculous.

Oliver's navy and white striped outfit hung beside it. Bright yellow embroidered pineapples stood out against the pinstripes.

Oliver pulled it out with a look of confusion. "What is this?"

"It's a romper," I answered, excited to see it on him.

"I thought those were for girls."

"They make them for both. This is a male romper. It gives extra room for your bits. And look," I pulled it out, showing him the side. "It has pockets!"

He gave me a girlish squeal, "Pockets! Pockets make everything better. Why do all girls obsess over pockets?"

"You don't understand because you're a guy and guys always have pockets but imagine wearing this," I motioned to the romper, "and not having a single pocket. That's how dresses and skirts used to be. Not to mention the pockets in some of our jeans are too small to use for anything bigger than Chapstick, so having pockets is a win!"

"It's a giant step towards equality," he joked.

"Shut up," I slapped him playfully, and he caught my hand, pulling me further into the room. He unwrapped my towel and pushed me back to sit on the side of the bed.

Kneeling in front of me, he said, "We're still living in the moment, right?"

"All day," I said.

"Great." His eyes dropped to my chest. "This bathing suit has been torturing me since the first time I saw you in it."

His arms reached around me to free the ties behind my back. Then his fingers trailed up to unfasten the knot at my neck. The fabric loosened, and he tossed my bikini across the room. He was still shirtless, so when he leaned in, his skin grazed mine. His mouth met the curve of my neck, and his breath sent a shiver through me. I tilted my head, giving him better access.

He reclined me back, his body on mine, and his mouth strayed, trailing down my collarbone and then to my chest where he stayed for a while. His teeth teased my nipples, and my body undulated against the blissful torture. My hands grabbed at him, sliding down his skin, trying to reach his shorts, but he pulled his hips away. His hands caressed my skin, and he untied the strings at my hips. I felt like I should object, but I wanted him to keep going.

He looked up at me. "If you don't like something, tell me."

"I don't like that I can't touch you," I complained, reaching towards his shorts.

"Not yet," he said. "I want to see how worked up I can get you."

"I'm pretty worked up."

He shifted his body, so he was lying on his side next to me. He propped himself with an arm, and his head dipped to press his lips to mine. As we kissed, his hand grazed up my thigh and slid between my legs. He barely touched me, and I jumped.

I felt I should be a little more self-conscious, but when he pulled back to look at me, I felt beautiful. When he touched me, I felt desired, so when his fingers ran down my seam, I pushed into him with a moan. He already had me so wound up, like a spring ready to snap and I realized his soft sporadic touches were just to tease me. I needed relief. I needed him.

"Oliver," I begged, and his fingers dipped inside.

"Fuck," I heard him groan against my mouth.

I was practically dripping for him, and he spread the moisture and found the spot that made me lose all sense.

"Oliver, it's . . . I'm . . ." I moved against him, writhing.

I arched my back as his teeth nipped at my nipples and his pace quickened. He added another finger, sliding it inside me, finding just the right position, and the blissful torture continued until my body shook, and my world spun. I cried out and moaned some gibberish, unable to form coherent words or thoughts.

I don't remember closing my eyes, but when I opened them, Oliver was leaning over me, watching me come back down.

"Oliver," I panted, worn out even though I didn't do any of the work.

He tilted my face towards him and kissed me. I held his face, never wanting to let go. I wanted to breathe his same air forever.

Addison was a fucking fool. I was supposed to stay in the moment, but I couldn't help the thoughts. Evan never provoked even a tenth of the pleasure I just experienced at the hands of Oliver. But it didn't quench my thirst. It only made me feel more dehydrated. I realized how dry my life had been, and now that I had a taste of his sweet water, I wanted the whole glass.

I pushed him over onto his back and rolled, so I was leaning over him, our roles reversed, but he protested when I reached for his shorts.

I pulled back. "Honest truth, if you don't let me touch you, I'm going to get mad." Part of me couldn't believe I was fighting him, but I wanted to return the favor, and I needed to see if I could make him squirm the way he made me squirm.

"Willa, I don't want you to feel like—"

"I want to," I interrupted, leaning in to kiss him. I pushed him back, straddling his hips, his shorts still frustratingly in place. I trailed kisses down his chest. I felt his shaft twitch against my stomach as I continued to move down his body.

"Helllooo," I said, gliding my chest down the rod beneath his shorts. I watched for his reaction, and when his eyes closed, I rubbed my hand along the fabric and then it dipped beneath the material, pushing the shorts down for better access. I kissed his abdomen before pulling back and wrapping my hand around his length. His size was intimidating. I'd barely begun, and there was already a drop at the very tip.

I wondered if Addison was good at blow jobs but reminded myself to stay in the present. My hand stroked its way up his shaft, and I leaned down to lick the very tip before I took him in my mouth.

He groaned, and his hand rested on the back of my head. I wondered for a second why guys did that, but then I started moving, sucking, teasing. His groans of frustration mixed with moans of pleasure. I didn't tease him for long, and his hand on my head gently guided me.

I could feel his release coming, but he still warned me, "Willa, I'm gonna . . . "

"Mhmm," I moaned, peeking up at him. His eyes were on me, watching me, and the look he gave made me hot all over again. I began moving faster, more aggressive and his hips jerked, his hand stilled my head, and his liquid was warm in my mouth.

I did this to him. It was the first time I'd ever wanted to give someone a blow job, and it's the first time I'd enjoyed it. I swallowed and looked up at him, wiping my lips.

He was still watching me and groaned a "Fuuuuck."

He seemed to study me as his chest rose and fell. His

look was so intense. His blue eyes appeared darker. His pupils so dilated. If I were a betting woman, I'd say Addison never swallowed. I usually didn't with Evan, but with Oliver, I wanted to soak up as much of him as possible, and the way he reacted, made me want to do it again.

15

OLIVER

I never wanted to leave this hotel room. Willa sat back on her heels, kneeling on the bed next to me. We had nothing between us. I realized her smooth caramel skin was her God-given color and not a suntan as I had thought. It was beautiful and gave her an air of mystery. I reached for her, pulling her up to lie beside me.

Her lips were a deeper shade of pink, and her eyes filled with passion. It was impossible not to compare her to Addison, which was ironic since Addison didn't compare to Willa.

If I had a ring, I'd be tempted to propose. Her dark waves hung over her shoulders and spread across her chest. I grabbed a curl, playing with the drying ends.

I wanted to say something but didn't have the words and didn't want to ruin the moment by saying something subpar. I settled on saying, "That was incredible!" The words weren't adequate enough to describe all I was feeling.

She leaned in to kiss me, and when she pulled away, she said, "I don't want to say the wrong thing and ruin this moment, so I'm going to kiss you again, and then I'm going back to my room to get ready."

I smiled against her lips, and held her against me, lengthening our kiss and delaying her from leaving.

Eventually, she pulled away. I propped my head in my hand to watch her naked hips sway as she retrieved the pieces of her bathing suit. Then she wrapped the towel around her, grabbed her things, and walked toward the door. She looked back at me and paused. "Mmm, I'm gonna stand here a moment until this image seals itself into my brain forever."

I laughed and said, "Don't forget your dress."

"Oh," she stepped forward, grabbed the dress, and then resumed her stance by the door, staring at me.

"Go," I said, "You're making me blush."

She shook her head, and then she was gone. When the door shut, I rolled over, burying my face in the comforter. This wasn't supposed to happen. She stood right here in this room two days ago telling me she didn't want to be my rebound and I made her my rebound, anyway. But I wanted to keep her. I wanted what we had to stick.

I flipped over, looking up at the ceiling and rubbed a hand over my face. I wanted to know what she was thinking at that moment. She'd been so skittish in the beginning, leading me to believe every time she left might be the last time I saw her. I hoped we were beyond that, but part of me wanted to go check on her.

I stood up, feeling panic at the thought of her leaving, but I was acting crazy. She was making me irrational. If I went to check on her right then, she might feel smothered. I had to trust that she was doing what she said she was doing.

I shook my head free of the tangled thoughts and went to shower.

Snaps belonged on children's clothing and only children's clothing. I was more convinced than ever after snapping up the front of my new glamorized adult onesie. No respectable adult wardrobe contained snaps or onesies, but today I had both. The navy and white vertical stripes were pencil thin and pretty unnoticeable as a backdrop behind the quarter-sized fluorescent yellow pineapples embroidered every four inches. There was a solid navy band around the waist, almost like the designer wanted to give the illusion that the top was separate from the bottom, but why? Why would anyone get such a hideous top and then think, "You know what would make this better? Matching bottoms."

The romper was more formfitting than I liked. The fitted short sleeves ended before my biceps began. The bottoms kept bunching up around my junk, and the shorts hugged my ass and ended mid-thigh, something I was not used to. Looking at myself in the mirror, I felt like a male stripper.

I pulled my hair back into a bun because that was the only way it didn't get in my way. I didn't particularly like it this long, but Addison hated it, and because she threw such a huge fit, the rebel in me told her I wasn't cutting it until the wedding. And now that there was no wedding, I could keep it long . . . or not, either way, it would be my choice.

I slipped my wallet into my pocket and wished for a bigger pocket. It barely fit, but I managed to snap the pocket shut. I opened a chilled bottle of Pink Moscato and headed next door.

I knocked, and she called, "Just a second!"

She opened the door and ran back into the bathroom before even looking at me. She was wearing a short blue robe and leaning toward the mirror with her mouth open as she applied mascara. When she finished, she spun to me. I posed, leaning against the bathroom doorjamb with my bottle of pink wine.

Willa bit her lip trying and failing to hold in her laughter. "You'll make some man very happy someday," she said when she pulled herself together.

I sucked in my lips and nodded. So, she noticed it too.

She added, "At least I won't have to worry about any girls hitting on you today. The Pink Moscato was a nice touch."

"I think I'm gonna need it." I took a drink and handed it to Willa. As she took a sip, I turned around to the closet and pulled her dress out of the clear plastic, asking, "Have you tried it on yet?"

"No, I didn't want to mess up such a lovely dress."

The dress was over the top. I ran my hand down the sporadic glittering gold sequins, over the gold lace and bronzed feathers to the thick line of feathers that hung from the bottom.

"It's so very formal," she said, attempting to pay it a compliment.

"It was the thing I wanted to see you in most."

"It's Lycra so it should fit over my hips, but it will be tight." She took another drink and then handed the bottle back to me.

"I'm fine with tight," I said.

She eyed me, taking in my romper again, "I see that. You look very comfortable in fitted clothing."

"Not really. It keeps bunching," I said, straightening out the shorts again.

"Oh my god, I don't even care that I'm going to look like a fluffy Oscar. I'm so excited to watch you walk around in that all day." Her smile was intoxicating.

I took a drink as she asked. "If we're both drinking, how are we getting to the winery?"

"Let me see your phone, and I'll order us a ride," I said, setting the bottle on the counter. "How soon do you think you'll be ready?"

"I'm almost done."

"You're a lot quicker getting ready than Ad—" I stuttered because we weren't supposed to talk about our exes today.

She smirked and walked toward me. "Who am I faster than?"

"My uh, Grandma, Adelina."

"Oh, are you close to your Grandma Adelina?"

She was standing so close. It was distracting. "She was my great grandmother, but I'm told we were very close for the first four months of my life."

She grabbed the bottle and took another drink. "That reminds me of my old Professor named, umm let's go with, Edwin. You see his ass," she reached around me to grab my ass with her free hand, "could never pull this off the way you do. In fact, he doesn't measure up in a number of ways." She released me and set the bottle down but didn't move out of my space.

"Is that so? Then I should tell you that you are on a different playing field than granny."

She made a face. "I'm a little weirded out by you comparing me to your granny."

I nodded. "Then why don't we move on and you just tell me when you're ready for me to order a ride."

I started moving out of her way, but she grabbed me, pulled me forward and in one go, ripped open the snaps of my romper exposing my chest down to the top of my boxers.

She laughed, saying, "Half the reason I picked this for you was for that exact purpose."

"You wanted easy access, so you dressed me like a gay stripper."

"That's homophobic."

"I'm fine with people's sexual preferences, but I'm not fine with being a tease by putting out the wrong vibe."

"I can't help how pretty you look despite your rugged manliness." Her hand dragged down my jaw. "Even with your unkempt stubble." Her eyes were on my lips, and she lifted her chin like she wanted to kiss me, but I wasn't giving in.

With her palms flat against my chest, she stood on her tiptoes, her breath tickling my neck. "Even with your long hipster hair and man bun . . ." She nipped at my lower lip, and I tilted my head forward.

She whispered against my lips, "I can't remember the point I was trying to make." She pushed up further on her tiptoes until her lips met mine.

I wrapped my arms around her, returning her kiss. After a moment, she pushed against my chest, and I loosen my grip. She stepped away from me, saying, "Stop trying to distract me."

"Me? You're the one ripping my clothes off."

She smirked, grabbing the bottle of wine. "This is going to be a delightfully fun day." She took a sip and started to move past me but stopped. "Wait, where are your shoes?"

I looked down at my sandals. "I'm wearing the only pair I brought with me."

"No, I bought shoes to go with your romper."

"You did? I didn't get shoes for you."

"That's okay. You bought me this lovely dress." She stroked the gold monstrosity. "Did they leave them on the floor of your closet?"

"I didn't notice anything, but I'll go check."

I went back to my room and looked through the closet. There they were, sitting on the floor covered with the clear dry cleaner's bag. I had thrown the bag from my romper on top of it without realizing they were there. Even with all the plastic, I don't know how I missed the neon yellow shoes. They matched the pineapples on my romper perfectly. We exchanged our sizes, and I looked through the shoe section but had no idea what to pick for her.

I slipped into the shoes, feeling like I was wearing high-lighters on my feet. I'd never worn pre-owned shoes, but these looked like they were brand new.

I went back to Willa's room. She left the door cracked for me. I opened it, and there she was wearing the gold dress, looking like a goddess. My eyes caught on the plunging v, giving me a great view of her cleavage.

"Will you tie the back?" she said, turning around.

I stepped forward. "It ties?"

"Yeah and thank God we can tighten the top. I can't wear a bra with this masterpiece, and if my boobs were any bigger, this dress would be inappropriate."

I grabbed the loose ends and pulled them together, but the dress wasn't laying right. "I don't understand how this is supposed to go."

She was laughing at me when she realized what I did. "I could've done that myself. You can't just tie the straps around my neck. You have to crisscross the straps. Then push them through the little loops."

"What loops?"

She tried to reach behind her back to show me, but I saw the tiny loops on the part that was gaping open. "Oh, I think I got it." I started pulling the tie through the little hoop. Once I had them through, I tied it. "Done."

"Oliver," she said through a laugh. She turned to face me with her hands holding the dress up over her chest. "Tie it tighter. If it's too loose my boobs will fall out. I don't need a nip slip."

"Now you're just being high maintenance, but fine. Spin back around." She turned, and I pushed her in front of the floor-length mirror.

"Oh my God!" she cried, shaking her head at her reflection. "We're gonna draw a lot of attention to ourselves today. Your shoes are amazing by the way. How do they fit?"

"Unfortunately, they fit well. I think it's only fair that we stop at a shoe store so I can pick out something for you." I pulled the straps until the dress covered her chest. "Is that good?" I asked before I tied it. "I feel like that is a proper amount of cleavage."

"A proper amount? It's fine, that's where it's supposed to go. Let me pull the girls up before you tie it."

She adjusted, and I tied. I stepped back to take her in.

The hem of the dress hit a few inches above her knee, but the fine feathers hung down to her kneecaps.

Her hands caressed the dress as she said, "I feel like someone took a lacy gold dress that was actually pretty and thought they'd spruce it up with things they had lying around in their craft room. Maybe they thought if the sequins were sporadic enough, they wouldn't be too much. But the feathers. Oh my. I feel like someone destroyed a perfectly good feather boa to decorate the hem of this dress, and then they had leftover, so they stuck them in with the sequins. I mean, why?"

"It's ahead of its time. Feathers are the future," I said. "The gold works for you. It makes you look exotic. And," I touched her waist, "it shows your curves."

"It's pretty tight, but at least it won't fly up with the wind."

I reiterated, "We're stopping to get shoes for you, and before you say no, we'll have to stop either way because I need socks."

"That's fine with me. But it's another place you'll be seen in your romper and those shoes, my God! I can't look directly at them."

"You have such amazing taste my fluffy duck."

"You're so sweet, like a pineapple upside-down cake."

I laughed and said, "I'll order that ride now."

16

WILLA

"This is our ride," Oliver said, as a blue Buick pulled up in front of the hotel. The guy driving the car did a double-take of us.

"Yep, we look hot," I said.

Oliver smiled at me as we walked toward the car. "Hot mess, maybe. He probably had to look twice because the glare from my shoes blinded him."

"We're just high fashion. Remember, we can't tell anyone why we're dressed like this or it will ruin the game."

"It's a game now?"

"Yep," I said as he opened the back door.

"Hey, Collin, how are you, man?" Oliver said like he and the driver were best buds.

"Doing good," Collin replied. "This looks like it's gonna be a fun ride."

"We're going to a winery!" I said, excited and a little tipsy after drinking most of the wine Oliver brought over. "And he's going to buy me shoes to go with my dress. It's designer, you know."

Oliver laughed, "I've never seen someone so excited over a dress."

Oliver and Collin chatted a bit while I stared out the window thinking about how weird life could be. Here I was in a different state, in a stranger's car with a man I'd only known for three days but felt like I understood better than I ever understood Evan. He was going to buy me shoes, and suddenly I felt like Cinderella with her glass slippers. Would all of this go away at midnight? We said we were living in the moment today, but what about tomorrow, and the next day? I was falling for Oliver, and I knew it wasn't smart, but I had the feeling he was having the same thoughts about me. But what if I was wrong? Or, what if I was right, and this was real and not just a crazy fling? What if he was my happily ever after?

"Oliver," I said, almost panicking over my own thoughts. I needed him to drown them out before I got sucked under by my doubts and fears.

He broke his conversation with Collin, saying, "Yes, duckling."

I fought my smile and grabbed his hand, lacing our fingers together. "You are the pineapple of my eye."

He smirked, and to Collin, said, "Yeah, let's try that shoe store you were talking about."

"What shoe store?" I whispered to Oliver.

"Collin said there is a shoe warehouse that has thousands of shoes, and it's only a few minutes out of the way."

"Thousands?" I said, "That sounds intimidating."

In fact, it was intimidating. We entered the store, which felt very much like a warehouse with racks and racks of shoes filling every inch of the place.

Oliver commented, "I see where they got the name."

"I see women's shoes over here," I said, pointing to the right.

Women's shoes didn't seem to have any order to them, with tennis shoes next to heels and boots with sandals mixed in everywhere. Oliver was looking at stiletto heels.

"Oliver, we might be walking through grass. Those heels will sink, and spikes aren't good while drinking. I'll end up looking like one of those girls from the bachelorette party."

He set the heels down and moved on. He held up a stray gladiator sandal, and I cringed. The straps were knee-high, and they had quarter-sized rhinestones down the front. "These are sparkly," he said, turning toward me.

"They sure are. What size?" I was praying they weren't the right size.

"Damn, these are too big. They might have more somewhere."

"God, I hope not," I grumbled.

We made our way down one aisle, then the next, passing shoes that would have gotten the job done, but apparently, he felt they weren't as awful as his shoes.

"Here!" he said, holding shoes up to see if they matched my dress. They were beige thick heeled sandals with thin straps and tan fluffy feathers covering the thin straps. "They're the perfect color, and they're your size. Put 'em on. Put 'em on," he sang.

He was too excited. If these fit, then I'd have feathers covering my feet instead of rhinestones up my shins. I didn't know which was worse. I sat down on a bench, slipped out of my sandals, and slid the fluffy shoes on my feet. The delicate feathers swallowed my feet, concealing everything but my toes. They tickled my feet a little, but they were comfy enough.

I stood and sashayed down the aisle and back. "What do you think?"

"I think we have a winner."

"I feel like I have bugs crawling across my feet," I said as the feathers shifted on my feet. "I'll have to get used to that."

He held out the box the shoes came in, and I took the shoes off and placed them inside, catching the price. "Holy shit! These are ninety dollars, Oliver. We can't get these!"

Oliver smiled. "We aren't getting them. I am." He took the box toward the register, and I slipped into my shoes and ran after him.

"Oliver!"

"I'm getting them, Willa," he said.

"It was supposed to be a cheap thrift store thing, not a ninety-dollar new shoe thing."

He turned to me. "Watching you all day is worth more than ninety dollars. I'm getting them."

"Fine," I huffed, "But I'm getting your damn socks."

"Fine."

We walked out of the shoe warehouse, me having spent eight dollars and Oliver having spent one-hundred. It felt pretty uneven, but that's how it felt like it had been going. Oliver always got the raw end of the deal.

Collin waited for us because Oliver offered to pay him double if he stayed. I climbed into the car, and as soon as Oliver got in, I asked, "Are you rich?"

He responded with, "I do alright."

I laughed, "That's a wealthy person's humble way of

saying they make a lot of money." I looked up to Collin for back up, saying, "Am I right?"

He nodded hesitantly.

I nudged Oliver. "See!"

"Way to put him on the spot," Oliver chided.

"He didn't have to agree with me. You're the one paying him, especially now that I know you make bank, and I'm living on a lowly teacher's salary."

Oliver rolled his eyes. "People put too much importance on money."

I laughed. "Says the guy who has money."

"You make it sound like I'm a millionaire."

"Shut up Richie Rich and give me my new shoes."

I changed my shoes and swung my feet up into Oliver's lap. I held one foot up, asking Collin, "What do you think of my new shoes? Oliver picked them out for me."

"They match your dress."

"That was very diplomatic of you," I said through a laugh. "My feet look furry."

"That's my little Ostrich," Oliver said.

"I might look like a bird, but at least I don't glow in the dark."

"So, what's the deal with you guys," Collin finally said, "Is this some kind of dare or something?"

I laughed, explaining, "We thought it'd be fun to pick out each other's attire for the day. So, I picked a fun Romper for him, and he picked out this golden atrocity for me."

"This is not a fun romper," Oliver interjected, "It keeps bunching, and it's too short."

"It's not that short," I said, thinking I could have gone shorter.

He looked to the front of the car at the same time he tried to tug his shorts down a little. "Collin, are these shorts too short?"

Collin looked back in the rearview mirror at us. "They are pretty short."

"See, Collin agrees."

"Only because he knows you're the one paying him," I said.

Collin laughed.

"Crap!" I said, "What am I going to do with my other shoes?"

Collin spoke up, saying, "I'm driving all day. Just put them in the trunk and text me when you're ready for a ride back."

Oliver said, "You'd do that for us?"

"Yeah," Collin admitted, pulling into the winery. "I want to hear how this goes for you guys."

Oliver got his phone number, and then we stepped out of the car, put the shoes in the trunk, and waved goodbye to Collin like we were the best of friends.

I turned to Oliver, and he was already looking at me, He held out his elbow, "Ready, duckling?"

I looped my arm through his. "Can't wait, glow-worm!"

The place was abuzz with people, and everyone aside from the staff wore casual summer attire. Even Oliver wore casual summer attire, but I looked like I was ready for a night in Vegas.

"I am so overdressed," I whispered.

"You better think up a good story for why you're dressed so spectacularly," he whispered.

"Oh, I'll think of something," I had to beat him to it. I bet he was coming up with a story about me already.

People were beginning to notice us, and I was way too sober not to notice the sideways glances. I needed a drink! We were escorted back to a bar where we sampled wines, and people gave us a wide berth.

"Let's get a table," I said, wanting to hide.

"Okay, but before we do, let's break the ice. Either we make everyone our friend or they will keep looking at us like we're insane. Let's make it a game. We take turns starting conversations with strangers, and after a minute or two, we rescue one another by using one of our cute nicknames. Like I would say, 'there's my fluffy gold star,' and you would say, "My lemon drop, where have you been?'"

"That could be fun."

He added, "If we can't come up with a nickname or if we make it too obvious, then we have to down our glass or take a shot."

"So, essentially you're proposing a break-the-ice-with complete-strangers drinking game."

He grinned and nodded. "Yeah, what do you say?"

I shrugged. "Why not?"

Oliver emptied the bottle of wine we ordered into our oversized wine glasses, and we clinked them together. "May the best man or woman win."

Oliver turned and walked across the room to a group of four women who looked to be in their sixties. They were gathered around a bar top table that overlooked the vineyard below.

"That's an interesting choice," I said into my glass as I took a sip, watching him work.

He was charming and had them all captivated. He looked so confident and comfortable, and I knew I was going to lose this game. I didn't want to interrupt him because then it'd be my turn, but I also didn't want to sit there alone, so I crossed the room, coming up behind him to slap his ass. "There's my ray of sunshine."

He turned toward me, and I couldn't tell if his surprise was real or not, but his face lit up when he saw me, and he said, "There she is, my glittering ballerina. I was just telling these wonderful ladies about the fundraiser we just came from."

I played along, "Oh!" I looked around the table, smiling. "It's such an important cause. We really ought to do more."

"I was bragging that you were the founder of the children's spelunking foundation."

My face felt hot, and I stumbled over my words. "It's just so important that every child gets down in those caves."

Oliver kept going, "I told them how important it was for the children but tell them the other reason."

What was he doing? I had just started to take a sip and instead drew it out, sipping very slowly. I lowered the glass and swished my wine before swallowing. "Mmm, you can really taste the oak in this one." I was talking out my ass. I had no idea. Oliver cleared his throat, holding in his reaction to my bullshit. Apparently, I got it wrong.

"Plastic," I finally said, latching onto a world problem. With confidence, I said, "Every child should have the opportunity to see the caves before they fill up with plastic. People are cleaning up the oceans, and all those plastic bottles aren't just going to disappear. They have to go somewhere and where better than hidden below the earth. We have to stand up and protect our caves."

"See," Oliver said, putting his arm around my shoulder. "What'd I tell you? She's amazing."

The woman nearest me, said, "That's a lovely cause."

Maybe these women were drunk because they seemed way too accepting of such a ridiculous charity.

The women across the table said, "Oliver, you're right. She did an amazing job. You didn't give her much to work with, but she pulled it off."

I tried to hide my confusion until I understood.

Oliver looked down at me, smiling as he squeezed my shoulder, "I might not be very good at lying. These women cracked me right away. I told them I failed, and that you were way better at improvising."

"And honey, you were amazing," the women closest to me said, squeezing my hand.

I released a breath. "I wondered why you were all so accepting of the children's spelunking foundation."

That got me a few laughs which softened the blow from Oliver's deceit. It was stupid that it upset me at all, but I felt a little betrayed.

Another woman said, "She will beat you at your own game."

"We'll see. It's your turn my sparkling gemstone."

I looked at his glass. "You'd better drink that because you lost. You're going down my big fruity man." I turned to the table. "It was great to meet you all. Now, I'm going to show him how it's done."

I walked away with way more confidence than I felt. The place was pretty packed, which was surprising for a Thursday, but I guess this was a common vacation spot.

I debated which table to approach and narrowed it down to two. It was between the table filled with women my age or the table of men. Girls could be mean, but I was better at handling mean girls than I was at understanding most men. Oliver was the exception, probably because he had been so sad and honest. These guys were laughing, and so I went to the table full of women.

I approached awkwardly and set my glass on the corner of their table. "Hey ladies, can I bug you for just a second?"

They gave me looks that said they'd rather I didn't, but they politely obliged. "My friend Oliver just came out of the closet, and he wanted to come here to meet some guys, but he was nervous, so he convinced me to come. The only reason I'm dressed like a Vegas showgirl is because he didn't want to be the most awkward person in the room. So here I am, looking crazy and he hasn't spoken to a single guy since we've been here. I think he's self-conscious of his outfit."

They seemed to drink in the gossip, so I kept going. "He's a lot more comfortable with women so if you could compliment him when you see him, that'd be great. He's the one in the pineapple romper."

"Poor guy. You're a good friend. I'm not gonna lie. I was wondering about your attire."

"He said if I looked like a Vegas showgirl then maybe he could show off his inner girl," I said, milking it.

I felt a tap on my shoulder and heard Oliver say, "There's my golden angel."

I gave the women a pleading face before I spun to Oliver with a smile. "There's my bear chaser."

The quick crease in his forehead said he didn't understand, but he smiled at the women, and they all greeted him, a much nicer reception than I received.

"I love the romper," one women said.

"And that hair. You're too hot to be straight. The sexy ones are always gay," another one said.

Oliver slipped me a look, and I smiled as he said, "You ladies are too sweet. Is it that obvious?"

"You're definitely giving off a strong gay vibe."

I put my hand on his arm. "See, Oliver, they all accept you for who you are, and they don't even know you."

Oliver turned toward me, and his hand caressed my face as he deadpanned, "This doesn't mean we have to stop having sex, does it?"

I knew the look on my face had to convey surprise if not panic. I went with shock, putting my hand to my chest. "I can't believe you'd bring that up. I was in love with you, and all you wanted to do is watch gay porn!" I spun on my heel and walked toward the bar. It was his turn to embarrass me. I ordered a lemon drop at the bar because I had been craving it since Oliver brought it up.

Oliver came up behind me, setting his empty glass on the bar. He swept the hair from my shoulder and leaned forward, his face touching my neck while he rested his hands on the bar on either side of me. He had me trapped. Not that I wanted to escape him. I liked him right where he was. His breath tickled my neck, and I leaned my head to the side to give him better access.

"That was quick thinking, angel."

"I could say the same to you, my sweet striptease."

He whispered, "Bear chaser?"

"It means you like big hairy men."

He laughed against my neck, and I swear it was the sexiest experience of my life, sitting there on a barstool at a winery, with Oliver wrapped around me. I didn't give a shit what anyone else thought. I was primed and ready to have my way with him.

They delivered my drink, and as I grabbed the glass, Oliver ran his hands down my arms, whispering, "I can't wait for later."

"If you keep that up, you won't have to."

"I know you feel ridiculous, but you look really hot." He backed up a little, giving me room to breathe without inhaling him.

OLIVER

The warm breeze felt nice, and it brought with it the sweet, airy scent of the vineyards. The aroma reminded me of freshly cut fruit, a light sweetness rather than cloying.

We sat at a table on the oversized patio that overlooked the vineyard. Our table's umbrella shielded Willa and me from the afternoon sun. The waiter had just taken away our empty plates but left the charcuterie board behind because we were still picking at it. We had been at the winery for a few hours, and we were having a blast. We had already had an excessive amount to drink, so about an hour before we began sipping water along with our wine.

We mingled with a good portion of our fellow patrons, and while most of them thought we were nuts, some of them seemed to love us.

A band began setting up on a stage at the edge of the patio. It was next to the wide-open doors that led to the bar. There was a big grassy area next to the stage with a few picnic tables further out.

Willa said, "I dare you to get up and do the Macarena to their first song."

At some point in the last hour, we started daring each other to do random things. It started small but continued to escalate, and so far, we had each complied with every dare. I couldn't be the one to break our streak.

"Okay," I said.

The electric guitar began, and the tune was unmistakable. My head fell into my hands, and I took a breath.

"This should be fun," Willa taunted.

As the intro played, I scooted back in my chair and walked out to the open grassy area in front of everyone. I began the Macarena when they started singing, "She's got a smile, that it seems to me . . ."

It was a fast-paced version of "Sweet Child O' Mine", so at least I could match the pace to the song. I wanted to look for Willa, but I didn't want to see the rest of the crowd.

Then suddenly, she was right there in front of me, with her phone out, and her camera rolling.

"Oww, looking good, pinstripes!"

I shook my head as she continued to record. I put more shimmy into the dance, licking my finger before putting it on my hips.

She was laughing so hard that I knew her video would give motion sickness to all who watch it. Finally, she tucked the phone into the top of her dress and joined me in the Macarena.

The singer shouted to the crowd, "Come on, everyone, get out there!"

I laughed, surprised by how many people joined us. The women who thought I was gay, the older ladies who thought

Willa and I were the cutest couple they had ever met, and even some of the couples we had spoken to came out to dance. It shocked me when the group of middle-aged guys got up. They were here on a work retreat and seemed too macho to dance. Granted, they did a modified version, holding their beers and drinking the whole time.

Willa was jumping up and down, clapping as they joined. I fucking loved her excitement. I loved to see her happy. She turned that excitement toward me, and her smile penetrated my core. It knocked the wind out of me. My heart tripped over itself.

Like spotting a bald eagle in the wilderness, Willa's uninhibited joy was rare and magnificent to behold. I couldn't get enough of her. I was happy the band extended the song to give everyone a chance to get up and make a fool of themselves. It gave me more time to watch her dance.

The band continued with songs people could dance to, and Willa was showing me all her best moves, like the shopping cart, lawnmower, and bus driver.

One of the older ladies pulled me over to do some kind of cha-cha dance with her, and Willa was pulled away by someone else. Suddenly, all the women were passing me around, and I lost track of Willa.

"Relax, sweetie, she won't disappear," Hilda said. At least I think her name was Hilda. She looked to be in her late sixties, but she was getting down like she was twenty.

Hilda said, "You ought to marry that girl. I've never seen a happier couple. You're both a little strange, but it's obvious you're crazy about each other."

I pulled her away from the crowd, probably taking her words too seriously. "We've only known each other for three days, and we both just got out of serious long-term relation-ships. We live in different states and w—"

"I don't know your situation," she interrupted, "but all I hear are excuses. Life goes by too quickly, dear. My husband died last year, and if we wouldn't have been so stubborn at the beginning of our relationship, then we would've had another year together."

I stared at her. I couldn't be taking her seriously. But I was. "What if I hurt her? She's already been through enough."

"Then don't hurt her," she said, making it sound easy. "Love her."

I shook my head "This is crazy."

"Life goes too quickly, Oliver, and the craziest things people have done were for love," she said, pinching my cheek. "Now, I've gotta go give my seventy-year-old knees a break."

While she headed back to her table, I turned to search for Willa. When I didn't see her anywhere, I went toward the person I saw her dancing with last, but before I got there, I heard, "Hey, my big sexy cocksucker!"

I spun, and Willa was running toward me with her shoes in her hand.

I laughed, "That wasn't subtle."

She was laughing and breathless by the time she got to me.

"Easy my sparkly feather."

She caught her breath and said, "I requested a song."

Just then, the lead vocalist of the band announced, "I love this crowd. We got an unusual request, and folks we aim to please. So, without further ado, I give you Cole." He waved a hand at the guitarist who had taken the lead position.

I was holding my breath, and my heart was pounding. Then the lead singer came back and said, "Guys, he's just going to wing it."

The guitarist shook his head, and the song started. I looked down at Willa. She was already watching me, waiting for my reaction.

"The fucking "Chicken Dance"? What is wrong with you?"

She tossed her shoes and offered her hand. "May I have this dance?"

I took her hand and stepped forward, saying, "Always." We danced our asses off.

When the song ended, Willa said, "Life would be a lot more fun if we weren't always so afraid of embarrassing ourselves."

She made a good point, and I was about to tell her so when she said, "I need water!"

We picked up her shoes on the way back to our table, both parched from dancing outdoors on a summer day.

We sat next to each other at our table as we rehydrated. I stared at Willa as we drank. Even with the sheen of sweat, she looked stunning and impossibly fresh like her sheen was from the morning dew rather than sweating her ass off. Her fitted gold dress showed every curve of her body, and she tossed her dark waves, looking sexy. I wanted to slide my hands into that hair, over those curves. I wanted to taste her. I wanted to hear my name on her breath as I was buried inside of her.

"I feel like you're undressing me with your eyes," she said, setting her glass down.

I set my glass down and nodded because that's exactly what I was doing. I still had the image of her from this morning burned into my memory.

"You have to be hot," I said, "We should probably get that dress off you."

She smirked. "It sounds like you're the one that needs some cooling off."

She was absolutely right.

"Hey, you lovebirds," Hilda interrupted, coming to stand by our table. "Let me take a photo of the two of you. I wish Richard, and I would've taken more pictures together over the years."

Willa pulled her phone out of her dress. I'd offered to carry it for her, but she said she didn't mind.

Willa wiped the sweat from her phone onto my romper and got the camera ready, handing it to Hilda. We posed for a few photos and then Hilda said, "Up, up. We have to get one with your lovely ensembles."

We stood, and Willa slipped back into her shoes and then we posed for one.

"Okay now one with you holding her, Oliver."

"What?" Willa complained.

I swooped her up, and Hilda took the pictures as Willa fought me.

"My ass is probably hanging out," she complained.

"No dear, there are too many feathers for that," Hilda reassured.

I liked Hilda. She reminded me of my grandmother even though she was closer to my mom's age. My grandmother always butted into my business, and it drove me crazy, but when she was gone, I missed her meddling. My mom never interfered with my life or tried to tell me what to do. Once I became a teenager, she basically stepped back and let me do my own thing. It's a wonder I turned out as well as I did. I probably would have been wild if it hadn't been for Addison.

I pulled myself back to the present and set Willa on her feet. She pushed away from me and said. "I'm going to run to the ladies' room. Will you keep my phone in your pocket?"

"Of course," I said.

After she walked away, Hilda asked, "Would you rather I hold on to it so I can take some candid photos? Candids are always the best."

"That'd be great."

WILLA

he woman who had just taken our picture came into the bathroom as I was washing my hands.

"Oliver seems especially taken with you," she said, acting like she had known Oliver for years. "In my opinion, you should take that boy home and marry him," she continued, coming at the topic with the grace of a piranha attacking my feet. I hadn't even realized I was dangling my feet in the water, just like I didn't realize this topic was up for discussion.

The shock must have been written on my face, because she said, "Oh, I'm sorry. My name is Hilda, and Oliver couldn't shut up about you. You two seem so crazy about one another. It makes me miss my husband. I hope you two are as happy together as Richard and I were."

"I'm sorry about your husband, but Oliver and I are not a couple. We only met a few days ago."

"I think that says a lot. It might be new, but you can't deny your connection runs deep."

Who was this woman? Rather than asking her to please, fuck off, I said, "I wasn't looking for Oliver, but we found each other, and we connected, but that's it."

"But that doesn't have to be it," Hilda said. "Oliver isn't the one who made you cynical of love, dear. Try not to punish him for it." She walked into a stall before she got a chance to see my anger.

What the hell! I looked in the mirror to straighten my hair, but thought, fuck it, and walked out of the bathroom. What had Oliver told this woman? I was going to find out.

The sun had crossed the sky since we first arrived and the breeze was blowing clouds in which cooled the summer air, but I didn't like the look of the dark clouds on the horizon. I wondered if they were coming our way.

I looked around for Oliver. He wasn't at our table or the bar, but I continued to search. Hilda had shaken me up. I didn't know if it's just because she made so many assumptions or because she made me question what Oliver was saying about me.

I finally spotted him over by the band. He was talking to the only female band member, and suspicions crept in. He was leaning so close to her, practically whispering sweet nothings into her ear. I choked, and my anger amplified. Men were cheaters. It was a fact I already knew. But I couldn't give Oliver that label because technically we weren't a couple. We hadn't needed to put a label on what was happening between us, and I hadn't wanted to, but seeing him whispering into her ear made me irrational. I felt deceived and possessive. I was livid—my day ruined. What would I do if he picked up another girl today?

Oliver turned toward me. We stood maybe thirty feet apart, and he beamed at me. I felt his smile all over, and my anxiety fell away. He walked away from the woman without a backward glance, squashing my reservations, and squelching my frustration at Hilda's meddling. He didn't look guilty because he wasn't doing anything wrong. He was probably talking into her ear because it was so loud.

This whole day had been filled with a joy that overshadowed my sorrow, but my insecurities almost ruined it.

His hands were behind his back as he walked toward me. His smirk was so big it made me smile.

"What did you do?" I asked him with a sense of dread.

Before he could answer the band announced, "We got another unusual request, and Andrea is going to help us out with this one." The girl Oliver had been talking to came on stage with her phone in hand, and the guitarist was looking at something on his phone while he practiced cord positions.

Andrea stepped up to the mic and said, "So we're going to slow things down a bit with this next song. Bear with us, you guys are really challenging us today, but I think we can make this happen."

The guitarist began, but she waved her arm for him to stop. "I almost forgot. This song is dedicated to the Pink fucking Moscato."

I smiled, and Oliver cheered next to me.

I had no idea what slow song Oliver would have picked out for us, but I quickly found out, and it wasn't slow at all. Or it wasn't supposed to be. I'd never heard a slowed down, acoustic version of "Wannabe" by The Spice Girls.

Oliver stepped in front of me. "May I have this dance?"

I looked up at him in awe and had to admit the band was rocking it. The woman's voice was smoky and soulful, giving the song a whole new feel. I laced my fingers through his, and we stepped out into the grassy area that had become our dance floor. We wrapped our arms around one another and slow danced to "Wannabe" for the second time in three days.

This time was sexually charged just like the first time. Only it was so much more because it wasn't just lust. My feelings grew every second that I was with him. "You truly are the highlight of my day," I said, poking fun at his shoes while also being completely honest.

His hand cupped my cheek, and he leaned forward. "Willa," he whispered, holding back.

I said, "Honest truth, Oliver. What's going through your head right now?"

His eyes searched mine. "I'm a sensible person, Willa, but when we're together, I forget to hold back. I know I wasn't supposed to fall for you, but logic never stood a chance."

I felt the same which is why I started to pull away. In my head, I knew he wasn't Evan. My heart ached for him, but fear was stronger than even my vital organs. It loomed over me, tainting every good thing in my life. I knew how to evade fear for a time, but I didn't know how to escape it entirely.

He pulled me back in, his hands gripping my arms, and we stood there staring at each other as people danced around us. "Tell me your honest truth, Willa."

"I'm too afraid," I said.

"Too afraid to tell me, or too afraid of your feelings?"

"Both."

"Face your fear, Willa. You said life was more fun when you weren't afraid to embarrass yourself. Imagine how great it could be if you weren't afraid of getting hurt."

"It's not that easy," I whispered, ashamed of my weakness.

He pulled me against him, whispering into my hair, "You are the bravest woman I've ever met. You've been through enough shit, and you've fought too hard to let fear win."

He was right. I was stronger than my fear. To let it cripple me would allow it to win and I had fought too hard to get to where I was. If I didn't move forward, then I'd be moving backward, and I would not cower.

I lifted onto my toes as I tilted my chin up. I wrapped my arms around his neck and kissed him. He kissed me back. Our kiss was public, and I was terrified, but his lips and tongue and roaming hands distracted me from my discomfort.

When he pulled away, he asked, "What do you want?"

"You," I answered.

He gave a shy laugh and said, "Well, that's good, but I meant are you ready to go back to the hotel. Do you want to get some more wine? What do you want to do?"

"I think we have enough wine back at the hotel. I want to get a bag of candy from the gift shop, though."

"You head to the gift shop. I'll pay the bill."

"Half of that is mine."

"Okay, then buy me a t-shirt, and we'll call it even."

I smiled, knowing that I would need to buy him more than just a t-shirt to make us even.

"What's that look?" he asked.

I spun to walk inside, ignoring his question and saying, "I'll meet you in the lobby."

⁂

THE BENCH IN THE LOBBY GAVE US A GREAT VIEW OF THE storm rolling in. The sunny day had cooled drastically, and the clouds and the gusts of wind were building. The band had taken a break and the patio had cleared. It was only four o'clock, but the sky continued to darken, looking more like dusk than a summer afternoon. No one had expected the weather to change. When I checked the forecast earlier, it showed clear skies all day.

I was scrolling through the new photos on my phone while Oliver pulled goodies out of the gift shop bag I had handed him. "This is more than a t-shirt," he said, pulling out the matching shorts and slippers I bought for him. I also purchased two wine glasses, a unicorn corkscrew, and a bag of chocolates.

I held up my phone screen to him. "Who took these pictures?" I said, confused and stunned by the number of photos. They were all of us, dancing together, laughing together, whispering together. But the one I held up to him was of us standing by our table. My head was thrown back mid-laughter while Oliver peered down at me with a smile and a look filled with serine fascination. My heart and body warmed in response to his intimate stare.

Oliver took the phone from me and smiled at the photo without a hint of embarrassment. "Hilda took them," he confessed. "I thought you'd appreciate the memories, and I had to make sure we captured every angle of you in that dress."

He handed the phone back, and I wanted to say more as I looked back at the photo. I needed to confront these feelings, but Oliver went back to his bag, pulling out the unicorn corkscrew as thunder rumbled in the distance.

"You bought me my very own corkscrew!" he laughed.

"There is also a bottle of bourbon in there, so you aren't stuck with only the Moscato."

He put everything back in the bag and wrapped his arm around me, pulling me closer and kissing the top of my head. "I love it."

The downpour began. Large drops of water pounded against the roof, and cool air blew in through the patio doors as moisture filled the air. Someone opened the front door, looking as if they wanted to make a run for their car but paused when they saw the heavy rain pelting the ground. The patter of rain grew louder and rolling thunder shook the ground. I leaned into Oliver, enjoying his body heat, his scent, and his calm presence.

As the gusts of wind became stronger, they closed the patio doors, cutting us off from the storm. The man at the door made a run for his car just as Collin pulled up outside.

He pulled up under the awning and Oliver and I grabbed our things and made a mad dash for the car. I slid into the back seat and Oliver was right behind me, both of us damp from the angled rain.

"Crazy storm," Collin said.

I replied, "It wasn't even supposed to rain today."

Collin pulled out from under the awning and rain

assaulted the vehicle, drowning out our voices, making it difficult to carry on a conversation without shouting.

We pulled out onto the road, windshield wipers set to warp speed and I grabbed Oliver's hand, wishing we could just wait out the storm, but I was the only one that seemed worried. Oliver scrunched his eyebrows at me, wondering what was wrong and gave me a reassuring grin, squeezing my hand.

"How're you doing, Collin?" Oliver shouted over the storm.

Lightning cracked, sounding like an explosion and I jumped. I felt Oliver tense next to me. The road had Collin's undivided attention. We were on a two-lane highway, and I could barely make out the blurry lines.

"Should we pull over?" I asked.

"There is nowhere to pull off and the shoulder isn't big enough," replied Collin.

Then the sirens began. At first, they were difficult to hear over the downpour, but the sound increased as did my level of anxiety. I pulled my phone from Oliver's pocket to check what was going on. Collin turned on the radio.

The wind howled, and the car rocked as thunder rumbled. I felt the vibration in my chest, the same vibration I felt with fireworks, but instead of a pretty show, this was accompanied by sheer panic.

I tried to focus on my phone and finally found it. "Tornado watch," I called out. "And severe thunderstorms."

The car shook, and Collin said, "I'm gonna pull off into the grass."

He pulled off the road while I pulled up my weather radar app to see which way the storm was headed and to get an idea of how long it would take to pass. The storm clusters were scattered, but it looked like we might not have to wait very long which was a relief because a semi flew past us, shaking the car as a wave of water covered us.

I didn't feel very safe on the side of the road. Oliver pulled me closer to him, wrapping his arms around me and kissing my cheek. "We're going to be okay," he said.

I looked up at him, saddened by the idea of losing him. If we died right then, I would regret not getting to spend more time with him. I wanted to see where things would go, and I felt like together, we would be really great.

We might have met while we were both in crisis, but we were recovering faster because we had each other. I'd never been so raw around anyone. He had seen me scream at God, and cry while reliving my most traumatic moments. I didn't see my life taking this turn, but I was starting over, and I wanted to do it with Oliver.

When the rain began to lessen, I said, "This might be the best we get before the next wave hits."

The sirens were still going off, and now my phone was reading tornado warning, but it didn't look like the funnel cloud was in our direct line. "They spotted a tornado, but it's not close. How long is it back to the hotel?"

"Fifteen minutes," Collin said, pulling back onto the road.

"Collin you're getting double time for this buddy."

"Make that triple," I said.

"I didn't realize I would have to risk my life to come pick you up," Collin said with a laugh. "How was your time at the winery, anyway? Did people like the feathers?"

The tension in the car eased, and I said, "I got some kind words, but I think they were pity compliments."

"I complimented you," Oliver said, "That wasn't pity."

THE RAIN WAS STILL COMING DOWN WHEN WE REACHED the hotel, but the sirens had stopped. I insisted on paying Collin and sent Oliver to retrieve my shoes from the trunk.

"Seriously, thank you," I said to Collin. "Please be safe."

He assured me he was done for the day, and I got out of the car. Oliver closed the door, and we walked into the hotel.

We received a lot of looks on our walk through the lobby, and I had almost forgotten how ridiculous we looked. We boarded the elevator, and I admitted, "That car ride was the scariest of my life."

"What, you act as if you've never driven through a tornado before?"

"Well, excuse me for not being cultured. I guess I like to play it safe when it comes to mother nature and deadly machines."

He laughed. "Did you just refer to cars as deadly machines?"

"They are." We exited the elevator and walked toward our rooms.

"When I see a car, I have never thought, 'oh, look at that deadly machine.'"

"Shut up," I said, shoving him as he pulled his room key out of his pocket.

We bypassed my room, and he opened and held his door for me. I entered ahead of him. The lights were off, and the curtains were partly drawn. The light coming in from the window gave the room an unusual pink cast. Apart from the thunder rumbling in the distance, everything was quiet, and I was instantly more aware of Oliver.

He stood behind me, just inside the door. He dropped the gift bags, and instead of reaching for the light switch, he reached for me. He pulled my hair over my shoulder, and I leaned to the side. He placed feather-soft kisses up my neck to my ear, where he whispered, "I'm happy we didn't die."

I wanted to say *me too* but closed my eyes and moaned an agreeable noise. His hands on my shoulders, slid down my arms until they reached my hips. His fingers went to work on the ties of my dress, and I felt a shiver run through me. His lips met my shoulder, where he said, "If you want me to stop, just say so."

I never wanted him to stop, but I wanted to touch him. I couldn't from this angle, and when I tried to turn, he wouldn't let me. "No, no," he said, nipping at my neck.

If it was a reprimand, I wanted to be bad. I tried again to reach back and touch him, but he pinned my arms behind my back and walked me forward. I thought he was taking me to bed, but he stopped and turned us toward the floor-length mirror.

Oliver lifted his head to look at me in the mirror. He looked so damn sexy. His blue eyes were dark with desire. He rested his chin on my shoulder and said, "Do you know how gorgeous you are?"

I looked at myself in the mirror, surprised that I didn't immediately focus on my flaws. Instead, I saw the beautiful woman Oliver was seeing. I was no longer the sad woman I'd seen for years. My dark eyes had lost their perpetual sadness and instead shone brightly. The feather-covered gold dress accentuated my curves, making me feel sexy and exotic. My wild hair fell in mussed waves over one shoulder while Oliver tucked his face into the crook of my neck on the other side.

He let go of my arm, and his hands worked on the back of the dress. I felt the material loosening at the top, but the lycra material was tight at the hips, so the dress didn't completely fall away. Oliver's hands slid under the material at my sides, his hands wrapping around my waist. He pushed the dress down my body, over my hips and it pooled at my feet like a bird shedding its feathers.

Cool air touched my body, calling attention to my nakedness. I lifted my head from the bundle of feathers, back to the mirror. I wore nothing but feather shoes and nude lacy panties. I moved to cover myself, putting my arms over my chest.

"You should never cover yourself," Oliver said, placing his hands over mine. He pulled my hands away from my chest and slid them down my stomach to my hips. He left them there and slid his hands back up to cup my breasts. "Look at you," he whispered in awe.

It was erotic to watch his hands roam my skin. His right hand glided down my stomach to slide beneath the nude panties. They weren't my sexiest pair, but they were the only thing that didn't show through the dress.

If Oliver was bothered by the nude panties, he didn't show it. His hand dipped further until the material covered it. He groaned a sound of pleasure. His fingers slid between my folds while he used his other hand to tease my breasts. His fingers circled my nipples without touching them. My need for him grew, and the cool air no longer bothered me as my body heated, the flush visible in my cheeks.

"Oliver." I pushed my ass back into his erection. "I need to touch you."

His answering groan wasn't enough. I tried to spin, but he held me against him. "Stay still."

He moved around me, putting himself between me and the mirror. I was fine with that. Our mouths met in frenzied kisses, and I gripped onto him, needing him as much I needed my next breath. He took a step, guiding me back. I stepped out of my dress and kept moving with him until my back was pressed flat against the narrow wall between the bathroom and the rest of the space. It was directly across from the mirror, and I wanted to know why he wasn't taking me to bed.

He broke our kiss and fell to his knees in front of me. His hands singed me with their heat as they slid down my body. My fingers went to his head, and I pulled his hair from its ponytail. I ran my fingers through it as I felt his breath hot against my panties.

The heat sent a shiver through me, and then his mouth kissed over the material. It was pleasure and torture wrapped in one. It felt so good, but I wanted more. As if sensing this, he tugged my panties down and left me in nothing but my feather heels.

I caught sight of us in the mirror and holy shit! It was such an intimate experience. Seeing it all happen in the mirror was almost enough to make me orgasm. My hands were in his dark hair. His stubble rubbed the inside of my thighs. His breath sent a chill through me, and I arched back against the wall, my exposed chest peeked with excitement as color tinted my cheeks. As his tongue tasted and teased, I watched without shame, feeling the natural euphoric confidence that came with carnal desire. I'd never seen myself in the throes of passion before. It was sensual as hell. My libido had finally earned her overtime.

He lifted one of my knees and moved it over his shoulder, so he had better access. When he hit the right spot, I arched my back, my head falling against the wall. My eyes closed from the pleasure, but I opened them right back up, so I didn't miss a thing.

OLIVER

I didn't know that it would ever be enough when it came to Willa. The taste of her. The feel of her skin. The sound of her little moans. Those manicured nails scraping against my scalp, tangling in my hair, and holding me in place was all too much, but it wasn't enough. I held onto her while she arched into me, lifting onto her tiptoes. She was close, and I knew it was selfish, but I wanted to feel her orgasm while I was settled deep inside of her. I wanted to experience all of her, and even then, I didn't know if it'd be enough.

I unwrapped her leg from my shoulder, and she made a noise of protest. I stood up and held onto her, kissing her and wondering if she tasted herself on my tongue. She was so sweet, and I really needed her right then. I picked her up, cradling her. She kicked off her shoes, and I set her on the bed.

She propped herself up with both arms while I took a step back. I toed off my shoes and removed my socks. I looked up, catching her eye before I ripped open the front of the romper just like a stripper. She sat up, reaching for me.

I stepped forward so she could grab the romper and tug me forward. I loved it when she took control. I pulled the romper off my shoulders and pulled my arms out. It slid to the floor, and I stood there in my grey boxer briefs. She pushed her hands under the material to grab my bare ass. She pulled me closer as she pushed my briefs down.

I leaned into her. Planting my hands against the mattress, I lowered myself on top of her, devouring her plush lips as our mouths fused.

Her hand wrapped around my shaft, and she stroked up and down until it was dangerous to continue. I reached for the damn romper on the floor and pulled the condom from my wallet.

Once I had it in place, I fit myself between her spread legs and paused before entering. Her supple lips, red and swollen, beamed with erotic pleasure, and I wanted to extend this moment, but I couldn't wait any longer. I dove in and watched her body react. Her eyes fluttered closed, and she moved against me.

She was tight and hot, and I needed more, so I picked up the pace and strength of each stroke. She gasped my name, and her body melted, compliant and at my mercy.

I wanted to kiss her, but I wanted to watch her more. I pulled her to the edge of the bed and stood to give myself better leverage. "Turn over," I said, and she obeyed.

She was on her hands and knees in front of me, and I pulled her ass toward me and started right back where I left off. She pushed back into me, meeting my strokes. Her back curved like a stretching cat as her hands reached out in front of her to grip the duvet. With one hand, I directed her hips, while the other splayed between her shoulder blades and ran down her spine. I loved the shape of her and the dimples on her lower back.

I was too excited, and she was so wet and eager. I was going to lose it. The hand I had parked on her lower back wrapped around to her front. My fingers worked the sensitive bundle of nerves, and she stilled her hips and called out, as her body quivered.

Her pleasure sent me over the edge, and when the shock wore off, I discarded the condom and collapsed next to her. I tried to spoon her, but she rolled to face me.

We were both breathing heavily. Her hands cupped my cheeks, and she kissed me. It was warm and sweet. It wasn't frenzied or urgent. It was a lazy kiss like we had all the time in the world. And we did. We would have a future outside of this hotel room—outside of our heartbreak. We would make room for one another in our real lives. I'd make sure of it.

When she pulled back, she stretched, and I couldn't help but touch her skin. I ran my hand down her abdomen and stopped my fingers over the scars. "What are these from?" I asked.

"My surgery for my ovaries. My belly button has never looked the same," she said, sticking her finger in her navel as if to make a point, but I didn't see anything deformed about it.

"It looks good to me," I said.

"Easy for you to say. You didn't see it before."

I chuckled because she was being ridiculous and cute.

"Don't laugh at me," she said without conviction.

"I can't help it. I'm attracted to your brand of crazy."

"You're attracted to my crazy?"

I nodded because every time she said something brutally honest or acted totally bizarre; I fell for her a little more. "You're so refreshing, and I don't know that anyone has ever understood me the way you do."

She smiled and cuddled into me.

THE STORMS PASSED, BUT NEITHER OF US WANTED TO GO out, so we ordered in. While we were waiting for our pizza delivery, Willa wanted to take a shower. I joined her, and we had really amazing shower sex. I couldn't get enough of her, and I was afraid I might scare her away with my intensity. I know I was scaring myself.

Willa had gone to her room to grab a few essentials while I went for ice down the hall, filling the bucket from the room. Now, Willa was in my bathroom, drying her hair while I washed our new wine glasses in the sink.

When I finished, I carried them out to the little table by the window. I uncork a bottle of wine, fill both glasses, and set the bottle in the bucket of ice. When the pizza arrived, I set it on the dresser and placed the paper plates on the table.

When she came out of the bathroom in her robe, fuzzy socks, and beautiful curls, I was pouring wine into the glasses.

She stopped and stared, a small smile curling her lips. "How romantic."

"That's me," I said, "The king of romance with our paper plates and fancy pizza."

"I'll take this any day over going to a hoity-toity restaurant where they make you pay twenty dollars for a soda," she said, taking a seat.

WILLA

It was the perfect evening. We ate our pizza and sipped wine. We were beyond playing twenty questions, and our conversations moved comfortably from one topic to the next.

When we finished eating, we moved to the bed and watched a movie. I fell asleep against Oliver's chest, but woke after the movie had finished when Oliver arranged us. We were lying together with my head tucked against his shoulder and my hand resting on his chest.

He covered us with the blanket, and my palm slid down his chest to the hem of his shirt. He tilted his head toward me when he realized I was awake. I ran my hand up under his shirt to feel his skin.

It'd been so long since I slept in bed with someone and somehow this act felt more intimate than sex. His hand moved on my arm, and he lifted my chin up to him. He kissed me once. It was gentle and lingering without a hint of lust. It was meaningful, speaking of more than sexual desire.

He turned onto his side, so we were facing one another.

He cupped my face between his palms and smiled at me; my love reflected in his eyes. It was sincere and powerful.

He leaned in to kiss me, and his hands roamed, finding nothing but skin beneath my robe. His hands were lazy in their movements, savoring the moment.

He lifted up, his body hovering over me. He peeled his shirt off with unhurried anticipation. His shorts came off next and then it was just us, skin to skin with nowhere to go.

Our hands explored, touching, feeling, without words because our eyes spoke for us. He slid back under the covers with me, and I rolled over to straddle him. When I had him posed between my legs, I whispered, "I don't want barriers, Oliver."

He knew what I was saying. No condom. "I'm on birth control, and I'm clean," I clarified. "And I already know your history."

He didn't stop me, and with no further protest, I lower my hips and let him fill me. I was motionless, taking the time to welcome his magnificent presence.

He whispered my name, and his fingers ran through my hair. I started rocking against him, slow and steady, delighting in the sensation.

His hands skimmed my body, from my breasts to my hips and back up again. He watched me with intense fascination. Then he rolled me, so I was lying on my back, and he was over me, letting me feel his weight without crushing me. He continued our leisurely pace.

We had sex when we got back from the winery. We fucked in the shower. But this was neither of those. This felt a lot like making love, and I couldn't remember the last time I made love, but it had never felt like this.

Oliver kissed me, our tongues tasting and relishing in one another as he drove into me over and over, slow and steady. His face fell to my shoulder, and he whispered in my ear, "You feel incredible, Willa. I will never get enough of you."

His pace increased at my moan of pleasure, and he pumped faster, stronger, deliberate. His strokes said I love you. The kisses he rained down my neck, screamed, I adore you.

Drenched and needy, I felt every stroke like it was a mini orgasm. His release came, and the pleasure on his face was beautiful.

He relaxed on top of me, and I loved his weight. I felt safe, like nothing in the world could ever hurt me so long as Oliver was there to protect me. He understood me better than Evan ever had, and sex with Oliver was addicting.

We cuddled for a little while, and I wanted just to lie there next to him and fall asleep, but eventually, I said, "In romance novels and movies couples always snuggle and fall asleep after sex, but that's not real life. Every woman knows to pee after sex. I get that it's not sexy to talk about, but you know what else isn't sexy? Urinary tract infections."

Oliver's laugh was soft but deep, vibrating like a purr of contentment.

I didn't want to get out of bed. I didn't want to detangle our limbs, but I pried myself away and went to the bathroom.

When I crawled back in bed, Oliver pulled me in, spooning me, and I fell asleep almost instantly. I must have rolled onto my stomach because I woke a little while later when Oliver's fingers made featherlight circles on my back. He kissed the spot below my left shoulder blade and laid his head there, whispering, "Birdie can keep her spot. But I'm claiming this side."

"Mmm," I moaned so he knew I heard before sleep pulled me back under, I heard him say, "I expect my own tattoo."

21

OLIVER

I woke to the sound of knocking. Willa was next to me, and she was blinking the heaviness of sleep out of her eyes as I propped myself up. I stood and searched for my boxers while Willa's sleepy voice said, "Who the hell is pounding at the door at . . ." she leaned over to look at the clock, "seven o'clock."

"Go back to sleep. I'll take care of it," I said as I slipped into my boxers.

From the other side of the door came a feminine voice, "Oli, are you in there? I really need to talk to you."

I looked at Willa who was now wide awake, looking at the door like it had grown horns and a devil's tail.

"Oliver, please," Addison begged, sounding beyond desperate. I knew what her tones meant, and this one hurt me. Part of me would always care about her, and I couldn't ignore the misery I heard in her tone.

I rushed to the door, opening it a crack.

Her clothes were the only part of her that looked like the Addison I knew. She never had a hair out of place, but today, her golden hair was a mess, her eyes were puffy and her face blotchy. It broke my heart to see her this way.

"Addie, what are you doing here?" I asked.

"Your phone is dead or off, but I have to talk to you, so I followed your credit card charges," she answered.

"That's not what I asked. Why are you here, Addison?"

"Can I come in?" she asked, placing her palm softly on the door.

I sighed. "How about I meet you in the lobby in a few minutes, and we can talk?"

"Okay," she said in quiet dejection, wiping a tear as it fell.

How could she be so upset when she's the one who wronged me? I did nothing wrong, but I was second-guessing all of my decisions.

I closed the door between us, and when it latched, I rested my forehead against it. I took a breath, reminding myself of why I was here in this hotel. I couldn't let Addison confuse me.

I turned toward Willa. She was propped up in bed with an arm holding the blanket over her chest. Her eyes glistened with unshed tears, and she swallowed, giving me a woeful grin. It was as if she'd already accepted the loss of us.

22

Oliver stared at me from the doorway, his face a mixture of sadness and regret. Would there ever be a man who wouldn't regret getting involved with me?

Failure never became easier; I simply grew better at hiding my disappointment. I'd trained myself to breathe through each defeat, and even though I knew to expect the worst, hope was a pesky bastard, always wanting, always telling me something good was just ahead.

Now, I sat there pretending I wasn't hurting as my latest failure stared me in the face. Oliver's past had tracked him down, and the look on his face told me he was not done reminiscing. I had given him the ability to hurt me, and he hadn't wasted any time, but I wasn't about to show him weakness. I swallowed back my tears and smiled at him, telling him I understood.

"It's okay, Oliver. I know you need to talk to her. I get it. Part of you still loves her, and you need to hear her out."

He shook his head, coming closer, "Willa, I don't love her. Not anymore."

I didn't believe him for a second. How can you love someone for eleven years and stop cold turkey? I think his feelings had changed, but it was evident he still loved her; otherwise, he wouldn't have been so upset.

I was fine with him still loving her. I was fine with complicated feelings. I knew life wasn't simple, and I would have let it play out, but honesty was vital, and he broke our one rule.

He lied to me.

He took a step toward me. "I just need to clear the air, Willa."

Maybe he didn't understand his emotions. Perhaps he didn't mean to lie. I could give him another chance.

"That's fine, really. Feelings are tricky. It's okay to be confused," I said, catching his face in my hands as he leaned forward to kiss me.

Our kiss lacked the passion that had been there the night before. When he pulled away, he said, "I swear to you, I'm not confused, Willa. I know what I want. Will you stay right here and wait for me?"

I nodded, a convincing lie. My first lie.

Lying wasn't difficult for me. I lied to myself all the time, but there was no way I would wait for him. I would go to my room and pack up so when this ended badly, I wouldn't have to leave anything behind.

He got dressed and kissed me again before leaving the room, promising to be quick. He was either a terrible liar, or he had his head so far in the sand, he couldn't see what was going on.

I had heard her voice, pleading and urgent, and I'd bet my car on the fact that she never called off the wedding. As soon as Oliver left, I pulled up Facebook and stalked Addison's page only to find out I wouldn't be losing my car, but there was a good chance I would lose Oliver.

I collected my things from Oliver's room and went next door to my own. I dressed and packed in record time, doubting myself every step. I couldn't let her manipulate him. I couldn't let him go back to her. Oliver was worth fighting for, even if he had lied to me.

I'd load my car and then wait to see how things played out before leaving. I rolled my suitcase off the elevator and into the lobby.

It was busy with people coming down for breakfast. Several people were checking out, so I took a seat in a comfy chair in a little out-of-the-way nook surrounded with plants. It gave me a full view of the lobby while providing me some camouflage.

Oliver and Addison sat across from one another at the same table where Oliver and I ate yesterday's breakfast. Two cups of what I was sure to be green tea sat forgotten on the table as Oliver and Addison leaned forward with their hands clasped together on the table between them.

If he didn't love her, then I wasn't infertile. He gave her a look filled with so much adoration that my heart ached with the loss. I was so good at pretending, but I couldn't pretend he had looked at me that way. Whatever I had thought we'd had was nothing compared to what the two of them shared. How could it be? They had eleven years to our three days.

At first, I thought I would wait to say goodbye, but it hurt to watch him be so intimate with someone else. She held Oliver's undivided attention. He was looking and listening to her like she was the only woman in the world. She had tears leaking from her eyes, looking beautiful even in her sadness. Then Oliver slid out of his chair and came around the table to kneel, so he was level with her. He leaned forward and kissed her, their arms going around one another.

I choked. My damn heart still holding out hope for a future with him. Even as they pulled apart, his fingers slid through her hair, and their eyes connected in such an intimate way. I had to look away.

I used to be whole, but life had carved away a piece of me, like the cavity of a hollowed-out tree. And in that void, lived all of my lost hopes and broken dreams. Failed expectations nestled inside like temperamental hornets, stinging every so often to remind me of their existence. And on days like today, days when I kicked the hornet's nest, adding to my losses. All those past failures buzzed around inside, spreading their venom with each sting.

I had to disappear.

I grabbed my luggage and turned my keys in at the front desk. I wheeled my suitcase through the door, out of the hotel. I was almost to my car before I heard him.

"Willa, wait!"

I kept walking. I could forego loading the suitcase and just jump in the car and take off, except then I'd have to back over him. Damn it!

I was opening my trunk when he caught up to me. "Willa," he said, his voice pleading as he stood next to me.

"Addison will see us together," I warned as I loaded my suitcase into my trunk.

"I don't care," he said.

I slammed my trunk and turned to give him a look that said, *yeah right.*

"I don't," he repeated, shaking his head like he couldn't believe what I was saying.

"Honest, ugly truth," I said. "Did Addison call off the wedding?"

I already knew the answer but needed to see if he knew.

His shoulders slumped. "No," he said with so much regret.

"Are you going to marry her?" I asked, still holding myself upright.

"I don't know."

I swallowed the sharp needles of rejection he fed me. I needed to escape this torture, but I froze as those spikes I'd ingested tore me apart, irritating the damn hornets and causing a full-on frenzy. Every festering old wound reopened, and toxins poured out, filling me with so much anger and regret that the venom spilled from my mouth. "Did you tell her about us, Oli?"

He flinched, and I was feeling vindictive, so I kept going. "I get that you are confused, but how dare you let me think you were done with her. You made me the other woman, Oliver!"

He must not be used to disappointment because he did nothing to hide his pain, but I wouldn't feel sorry for him.

"Now, you and Addison are even," I said. "You are free to marry her without thinking you're missing out on other women. Glad I could help you clear that up."

"Willa," he tried.

I spoke over him. "I told you I didn't want to be your goddamn rebound, Oliver! You had women offer to be that for you, but I wasn't offering. You made me fall for you. Or at least the *you*, I thought you were."

I rounded my car and opened the driver's side door. I had refused to be his rebound but somehow became his mistress instead. And I hated myself.

"Willa, would you just listen?"

I turned to him, crossing my arms over my chest in preparation for what he was going to say.

"She . . ." He suddenly seemed unsure what to say next.

I helped him out. "She's the one you want."

"It's, well . . . fuck," he said in frustration as if words were suddenly the hardest thing in the world.

"Honest, ugly truth," I said. "I wish I had never met you."

His mouth gaped, and he stepped back, stricken.

I took the opportunity to climb into the car, slamming the door before backing out of my spot.

I drove away without looking back.

Who the hell meets the love of their life at a hotel, anyway? That only happens in romantic comedies and romance novels. The same world where UTI's don't exist and happily-ever-afters are only awarded to the people who deserve them. Real-life didn't give a shit if you were a good person. It would shit on whoever it wanted.

I wondered if Oliver would ever think about me. I knew I wouldn't be able to stop thinking about him, and that didn't seem fair. None of this seemed fair, but I already knew life wasn't fair, yet the injustice shocked me every damn time.

23

OLIVER

The grief took me off guard as I watched Willa drive away. My hands were on my hips like I was winded, and I kind of was. I couldn't breathe. I had fucked up. I'd screwed over the one person I swore I wouldn't hurt, and I did it so quickly. But what else could I do? Addison was pregnant, and Willa made it look so easy to let me go.

I stared at the road where her car had been, wondering how I could make this right. There was no right. *Right* would have been not sleeping with Willa. *Right* would have been not making her promises and painting a picture of our life together. The only right thing I could do for her is to leave her alone and take care of the woman pregnant with my child.

As I walked back toward the hotel, I saw Travis leaning against his SUV. Of course, he brought Addison here. No one else knew about the baby or the breakup, and Addison was in no condition to drive. I realized he'd just seen the whole production between Willa and me.

To my surprise, he didn't look smug. He looked miserable. We just stared at one another until I walked away. Willa was innocent, but the rest of us had fucked up. Maybe we deserved each other.

I could have been honest with Willa and told her about the pregnancy, but I knew it would have only hurt her more, and she still would have left.

I went back into the hotel, and Addison was standing just inside. I told her I'd be right back before I darted out the door after Willa. She had to know something was up, but she didn't ask.

I rubbed the back of my neck. "Let me go pack my things and we'll head out. You can go tell Travis that he can take off."

She looked nervous and placed her hand on my arm, "Oli, are you okay?"

I shook my head. "No, Addison. I'm not okay, but sometimes all you can do is tread water and hope one day your feet will find solid ground."

She dropped her hand and stepped back, unsure what to say to that. I didn't care what she made of it. It felt truer now than ever before.

I entered my hotel room and nearly broke down. It smelled like Willa. Everything in the room made me ache for her, and I suddenly realized I didn't even have her phone number or her full name. I knew so many intimate details about Willa, but we didn't exchange any practical information, like where we lived or our phone numbers. She had my information because she took a picture of my license, but she wouldn't be reaching out to me anytime soon.

I packed slowly, lingering in my regret. There were several remaining bottles of Pink Moscato, but I left them behind because it would always remind me of Willa, and I couldn't handle that right now. If I would have stayed that night and heard Addison out then none of this would've happened, but it did, and now I had to live with it.

I tried to shove everything in my backpack, but it wouldn't all fit. The bag from the winery gift shop was the biggest, so I stuffed everything else in it.

I checked out, and Addison and I walked to my truck in silence. We climbed inside, and I looked over at Addie and pictured Willa sitting there a few nights ago after our trip to the beach.

"Why are you looking at me like that?" Addison asked.

I shook my head and shrugged, before putting the truck in gear and pulling away from the last five days of my life.

"Did you sleep with her?" Addison asked out of nowhere.

I nodded, saying, "Yeah."

"Oliver, I know I hurt you, and we have some things to work through. I'm sorry."

She'd already said all of that. "I hurt her."

"Who?"

"The woman you saw me with."

"The one you slept with?"

I nodded.

She replied, "I'm sure she'll be okay. You couldn't have known each other that well. You've only been gone for five days."

Willa was strong. I knew she would be okay, but Addison was wrong about the other part. Willa and I knew each other. The short time didn't matter.

Before we got on the freeway, I pulled into a drive thru.

Addison looked at me, her eyes wide. "Oli, what are you doing?"

"I want a cheeseburger."

She looked shocked and hurt. "But, you. You don't eat meat or fast food."

"No, Addison, you don't eat those things. I do." I ordered my food and pulled around.

"But Oli, they're so bad for you." She hesitated on that last word as if realizing she shouldn't lecture me.

"So is sleeping with Travis. Do you even know how many times he's been treated for STD's?"

"Oli!"

"You think I'm kidding? I was legitimately concerned he'd catch something that antibiotics couldn't fix. You're the doctor. You know what I'm talking about. Hell, you probably wrote him a prescription or two."

I was acting terrible and unfair, but she didn't fight back. Willa would have screamed at me, calling me out for being an asshole, but Addison stayed quiet, turning toward the passenger window to ignore me. I didn't know if she was giving me the silent treatment or if she was angry with my words, but it turned out to be neither.

As I collected my food from the window, Addison wiped her face, and her shoulders shook, trying to keep her crying silent.

I was a dick.

"I'm sorry, Addie," I said softly and heard her sniffle.

She turned back to me as she pulled a tissue from her purse to dab at her face. "You have nothing to be sorry for, Oli. I know I hurt you."

"Why did it have to be Travis?" I snapped.

"Because he was always around. Do we have to talk about this?"

"I think we should."

"Why does it matter? I messed up, but I want to spend the rest of my life with you. You have always been there for me. We're going to have a baby together. I don't want to trudge up the past. I never meant to hurt you, and part of me wishes I had never told you because then you wouldn't be hurting like this."

"You wish you would have just lied to me for the rest of our lives?"

"Oliver, I want to stand in front of all of our loved ones tomorrow and publicly tell them how much you mean to me. I would do anything for you. If I could take it back, I would, but it's in the past, and it will never happen again. Do you believe me?"

"Yes," I said.

"Do you still love me?"

I sighed because as much as I tried to deny it; I did love her. It was impossible not to love Addie. "Yes. I still don't understand how you got pregnant."

Addison replied, "I'm surprised it took you so long to ask. I figured that would be your first question. I stopped my birth control a few months ago because it was making me gain weight, and I wanted to fit into my wedding dress. It wasn't a big deal because we were using condoms, but condoms don't always work. I don't know. Maybe your sperm are extra good swimmers."

"I can't believe you didn't tell me you stopped birth control. I would've been more careful if I'd known."

"It still could've happened. We don't know, Oli. Please,

give me the next two days. If you still want to call off the wedding, then we will."

"Okay," I said and then unwrapped my hamburger and ate it while I drove. To her credit, she said nothing else about fast food.

She had been up all night so a few hours into our trip, she fell asleep. She needed the time to sleep because rehearsal dinner started at seven and it would take nearly that long to get back to New York. It gave me a lot of time to think. I didn't know if I could forgive her for cheating, but it was difficult to stay upset with someone who showed so much remorse.

24

I was five hours into my trip home when one of my tires blew—nothing like a flat tire to add insult to injury. I tried to tell myself it could be worse, but I was feeling sorry for myself. I held the tears back as I called my dad to walk me through changing a flat. I successfully got the donut in place and stopped in the next town for a tire. They said they couldn't get the right tire until the following day, and I had no choice but to wait. I wasn't going to drive three hours on the freeway with a donut.

I stayed at a midlevel hotel, and the couple in the room next door were going at it like horny teenagers. It made me wonder where Oliver was at that moment.

Were he and Addison having makeup sex? Would he compare us? Would he think of me at all?

I don't know which thought hurt more and decided it didn't matter. I was the one to blame. I was a self-saboteur. I trusted another man and was fucked over again. It was enough to make me envious of lesbians even though I knew they had relationship drama just like everyone else.

OLIVER

Everything happened so quickly. Addison and I didn't have time to fall back into our normal routine because as soon as we got back to New York, it was a whirlwind to get ready and arrive at rehearsal dinner on time. With all the wedding plans, it was easy to forget the trip had happened. It was easy to ignore the unpleasant things.

No one besides Travis and us knew what the last week had entailed. Addison had kept everything on track, hiding our troubles from everyone. Part of me wondered if she was faking the pregnancy, but she showed me the five pregnancy tests she had taken, and I knew Addison wasn't a liar. She may have hidden the truth about her and Travis, but she never lied about it. I had a hard time believing she would lie about the baby's father, and she had offered to do a paternity test as soon as it was safe for the baby.

I hated that Travis had found out she was pregnant before I knew, but the bastard was there for her when I wasn't. I knew he loved Addie in his own way. I just never knew the feelings were sexual. I never knew he'd stoop so low as to sleep with my girlfriend.

Addison loved me. I knew she did, and we were going to get married tomorrow despite my reservations because logically it made all the sense in the world. If I called it off, I feared I would regret it for the rest of my life.

I had trouble distinguishing what I was doing out of love versus obligation. But in the end, I knew I loved Addison, maybe not in the way I once had, but I still loved her, and she was going to have my child. We were starting a family together. Other people would die for this opportunity, and I couldn't just throw it away. I had to give us a chance. If it didn't work out, then we would figure that out later, but for now, we would try to make it work, and to do that, I would have to stop thinking about Willa.

I got my hair cut an hour before our wedding rehearsal. My head felt naked without the long strands. It was still thick, but now it was only an inch or so long and my face was clean-shaven. With my dark hair coiffed just right, I put on the trendy suit Addison had laid out for me, feeling like a Cocktail Ken doll. All I was missing was an ascot, and I wouldn't put it past Addison to have something like that planned for me.

I felt like I was living someone else's life. Ever since I broke those plates with Willa, my eyes had opened to how passive I had been in my life. I'd let too many people make my decisions for me. It was easier for me to conform to their way than to form my own opinions, and I was okay with living that way until I met Willa and found out what it meant to experience life.

I needed to talk to someone, but I couldn't go to either of

the people I trusted most. I wished my grandma was still around because I could always confide in her. But without her, Addison, and Travis, no one was safe to talk to, not when everything was a secret.

Travis was still my best man, and he and I barely spoke the whole evening. I only found him beside me when it was deemed best man duty. He gave a convincing toast at rehearsal, and I believed that he loved Addie and me, but he also hurt us.

I smiled at the right times and went through the evening without incident. We were surrounded by good people who despite some superficial qualities, cared about us deeply and would be shocked and saddened if we called things off.

I stopped Travis before he could leave. He hadn't brought a date which was unlike him, but I wasn't surprised. With everything that had happened, he didn't want a date to witness the terror I could reign down on him at any time. I wouldn't do something like that to him, but the past week I'd acted so out of character that I didn't blame him for being nervous.

"Thanks for the speech and playing the part," I told him. "Then again, I guess you're used to playing the role of best friend."

He looked around. There was no one nearby, so he stepped forward. "Oli, I'm glad she told you. It's been killing me, but I didn't want to hurt you. I never meant for anything to happen."

"Why did it happen?" I asked because Addison had been evasive about the specifics, saying it would only hurt to bring up details.

Travis said, "My feelings for Addison have always been

complicated. She's my only female friend, and sometimes the lines blurred. None of us are perfect. We all make mistakes, and sometimes we hurt the people we're trying to protect."

His words made me think of Willa and how I had hurt her. "I'm not the only one you hurt. This hurt all of us, Travis, and it has fucked up all of our relationships. I don't think I'll ever trust you again and Addison is different, now. I miss the way things were, but we can't go back."

He winced. "I know."

"Standing here with you, I wish I could forget or at least forgive you." I shook my head. "But I don't know how. I know it's not all your fault, but I keep getting the urge to break your nose."

He smirked. "You should wait until after the wedding. You don't want to ruin pictures."

I almost laughed, but my anger overpowered his joke. I wish it was that easy to fix our friendship, but his humor stung. I missed his wit, and I knew it would take time and effort to resurrect what we'd had.

26

I pulled into my parent's house at two-thirty the next day. They lived on the same farm since they got married over thirty years ago. The blue ranch had a wraparound porch that was my mother's pride and joy. She was always sitting out there and yelling to my dad out in the barn who couldn't hear her anymore because he was half deaf. Bella jumped off the porch when she heard my car, and my mom stood from the porch swing, a lemonade in her hand.

I opened my car door and was immediately assaulted by Bella, who jumped in my lap and gave me kisses while her butt shook so hard it made her lose her balance and topple over, allowing me to get out of the car.

I gave her some love before getting my luggage from the trunk. She hopped alongside me up to the porch.

My mom had set down her lemonade and held her arms open wide, an invitation. I took the two steps onto the porch, dropped my suitcase, and fell into her outstretched arms, and even as much as I loved her, they weren't the arms I wanted around me. She wasn't Oliver. I hated him for making me fall in love with him. I cried into her shoulder as she held me.

My mom didn't know the whole story. She just knew that Oliver went back to his fiancée, but she didn't know all the in-between, and I wasn't in the mood to relive how insane I'd been. I just wanted to lie down in my own bed.

"I made Chicken Marsala for dinner," my mother chimed into my hair. "Your favorite. And there is pumpkin pie for dessert."

"Thanks, mom. You didn't have to do that," I said, pulling away and wiping my tears.

She held my cheeks. "You will always be my daughter, and when you've had a bad day, I will do whatever I can to make it better. Food always makes me feel better." She put her hands on her belly, "I guess that's obvious." She laughed a hearty laugh with an easy smile, and I wished I was more like her.

While I was growing up, people frequently asked if I was adopted. I hated the question, and I knew my mom didn't care for it. It was just that I didn't look like either of my parents. Not really. I was nothing like my mom. She had light hair and skin, a round face, and a sturdy figure. She was loving and boisterous while I was a shy child. I had more of my father's quiet humor and personality, but I had a lot of my grandmother's features.

My dad's mother was black, and his father was white. My dad inherited the light skin of his father and the dark hair of his mother. Most people didn't even know he was biracial, not that it mattered.

Then, enter me. I was born, and everyone wondered if there was a mix up at the hospital. No one expected my white parents to come home with a black baby. My skin wasn't all that dark, but it wasn't light either. It was enough to keep people guessing about my heritage, and it surprised me that Oliver never asked. I don't volunteer it, because I hated the term mixed-race or biracial. Weren't we all mixed-race? I was just a person who didn't want a label.

It had become a game to give obscure ethnicities whenever asked about my race. While filling out Bella's paperwork at the veterinarian's office, I was asked my ethnicity. I couldn't think of a reason why they needed to know where my ancestors came from, so I wrote Komondor, which is another name for a Hungarian Sheepdog. That was a year ago, and still, no one has commented on it.

I left my mom on the front porch where she went back to reading her book and sipping her freshly squeezed lemonade. I pulled my bag along with me while Bella led the way. I walked through the living room and down the hall where dozens of framed photos hung, showcasing my childhood. It was overkill, but it was also a reminder of how much my parents adored me. I entered my childhood bedroom, closing the door before I dropped my suitcase by the closet and sat down on my bed.

I thought I'd breathe easier once I was home, but this wasn't home. Neither was the house Evan and I shared. I needed my own place, and I needed to get ahold of my realtor to see how things were going.

I pulled out my phone to call him and after a quick chat found there was a bidding war going down. Apparently, it was everyone else's dream home, just not mine.

I would start looking for a new place tomorrow. Tonight, I just wanted to be surrounded by the people who loved me the most. Perhaps my parents gave me too high of expectations. They loved one another so much, and they loved me even more. Growing up, I may have felt lonely sometimes, but I never felt unloved. I was smothered by it and just assumed that love would carry through to my adult life. So, the shock of finding out that love was fleeting wasn't something I had been prepared for.

27

Oliver

I didn't back out. The morning went by in a scheduled blur of photographs and small talk. My parents looked so proud. Addison's mother cried happy tears as she patted my cheek before the ceremony. Addison and I were meant for each other. This was the way things were supposed to be. Everyone knew it.

At one-thirty on the dot, Travis patted my back to get my attention when it was time for me to walk to the front of the church where I would wait for Addison. Once there, Travis leaned in, asking, "You okay?"

"I don't know if I can do this," I whispered back.

"Oliver, I know you. If you leave her at the altar, you won't be able to live with yourself."

The bridesmaids came down the aisle holding bouquets of purple roses. Everything was beautiful. The flower girl laid the petals just like Addison taught her the night before.

The music changed, and Addison came down the aisle. Travis leaned in, whispering, "You can do this Oli. You love her."

Addison looked beautiful in her lacy fitted gown. She was gorgeous, and yet, I had no butterflies. Her father released her to me, and I took her hands in mine, trying to find those feelings I used to have, but they felt muted. Everything about her was dull in comparison to Willa.

Suddenly, I looked out in the crowd, wondering if she would show up and object to the wedding. I knew why I was doing this, but it felt so wrong. I was in love with Willa.

I was in love with Willa.

Addison tried to steady my hands as they shook, and tears came to my eyes. To the crowd, I looked like the sweet groom who was so in love that he cried at his wedding. And they were right. I was in love. It just wasn't with the bride.

Addison's eyes shimmered, and her eyes filled with fear. She knew. She knew I couldn't do this. Maybe she felt we had come too far to turn back—caged into our commitment by wedding deposits and guest lists. Wedding gifts had already been delivered to our house. But here we were in the middle of our wedding, crying because we were making the wrong decision.

She was begging me with her eyes, pleading with me to see this through. She was so scared I would abandon her on her wedding day and the embarrassment we would both face as our friends, families, and colleagues watched our relationship fall apart.

I loved Addison. She was my first love. She was a staple in my life, and I couldn't hurt her, so I hurt myself instead, the way I'd done for years, only now I knew what I was doing. Willa had opened my eyes. But I still felt a duty to Addison and now, our baby.

Addison and I recited our vows and said, I do. We kissed

and walked up the aisle holding hands as the room cheered. I tried to steer her toward an empty room, but we couldn't get away from people. The wedding coordinator ushered us around, keeping us busy talking to guests and thanking people for coming, but all the while, I kept wondering what we would do with our wedding gifts. What was wedding etiquette if the couple broke up before the reception?

We didn't get a chance to talk. People surrounded us, and we rode to the reception in a limo with the bridal party.

Our first dance was the first time we were alone enough to talk, but we had hundreds of eyes on us. I held her tight and said, "Addison—"

"I know, Oli," she whispered. "Just don't do this here. Please," she begged, tears in her throat.

At least she knew. We were deceiving everyone but each other.

I couldn't help it. I pulled up Oliver's Facebook page and witnessed everything that my imagination was telling me. He had gone through with the wedding. There were photos of the couple walking up the aisle as husband and wife. I wanted to say Oliver looked unsure, but it was most likely that part of me that was hopeful.

He had chosen her over me. I needed to deal with that. It would have been crazy for him to give up his love of the last eleven years to take a chance with a woman he'd known for less than four days.

The page refreshed and there was a photo of them dancing intimately. Their first dance. My nightmare.

I slammed the laptop shut and slid it across the desk. Papers scattered and some fell on the floor. I picked them up, coming across that damn baby shower invitation—the thing that started it all.

Had I not been so upset about the invitation, I wouldn't have felt the need to get away, and I would never have met Oliver.

I pulled the card out of the shiny thick envelop because somewhere along the way; I had turned into a masochist.

There was a handwritten note in with the invitation I hadn't noticed before. I unfolded it, and Evan's handwriting stared back at me.

Willa,

I know this might be hard for you to process. I don't expect you to come to the shower, but I didn't want you to find out from someone else.

I love you, Willa. I always will.

Oh, Hell no!

I didn't let myself think about it. All I had been recently was impulsive, so I continued my streak by gathering up the invitation and all its extra pieces. I grabbed my car keys and darted out the door. My parents were on the porch. They tried to speak to me, but I jumped in my car and peeled out of the driveway. I drove straight to the address on the return envelope.

Their house belonged in a storybook which only made me more bitter. It wasn't right that he cheated but still got to live his happily ever after, while I was left to suffer.

I don't remember getting out of the car, but the next thing I knew, I was standing on their big front porch pounding at the door, demanding answers. It took a while, but eventually, the door opened, and there stood Evan.

He looked the same as when he was my Evan, but he wasn't the same. He couldn't stand there and look at me with the face of my loving husband when he wasn't either of those things. I slapped him, hoping it would make me feel better.

It didn't.

I saw Estelle behind him, hiding down the hall. "Evan?" she asked, her voice hesitant.

He turned to her, saying, "It's okay, honey. Give us a minute."

She nodded and disappeared. Evan stepped outside, joining me on the porch. He closed the door behind him and turned to me. We stared at each other—neither of us knowing how to begin the conversation.

My anger fled as quickly as it had come, and I wish I could have hung onto it. When I wasn't full of rage, I was sad, and I especially didn't want to be sad in front of him.

I lifted the hand that still held the return envelope. I waved it in front of him, regaining a foothold on my anger. "A fucking baby shower, Evan!"

"Willa," he was shaking his head, regret, and sadness in his expression. "I didn't know how to tell you."

"So, you thought prettying it up with an expensive invitation was the way to go?"

"I wanted you to find out when you didn't have people watching for your reaction. I wanted to give you privacy to feel what you needed to feel."

"Then send me a text, Evan, not a goddamn invitation!" I wiped my tears away. I hated that I cried when I was angry. It made me feel weak, and I didn't want him to see weakness. I didn't want him to think he could hurt me. I didn't want him back, but I didn't want him to be happy either.

"Willa . . . " he choked, and I took a step back.

What the Hell? He was crying too. I didn't understand. I

shoved him, saying, "What do you have to cry about? You don't get to cry!"

"Do you think I wanted it to end this way?" he hissed.

"What? You didn't want to knock up the woman you were cheating on me with?"

"Don't bring Estelle into our fight," he said, and I knew I hit a nerve.

"Feeling mighty protective of your baby mama, are you? If our baby didn't die, would you put that much effort into protecting me?"

He looked pissed. "I won't listen to this." He turned to go back inside.

I wasn't done talking to him, and I needed to say something that would make him listen. "Hold on to each other while Jesus holds your babies." Saying the words made me lose my composure, but it got him to stop. "Those were your grandma's words to us before she died, and you promised her you would."

He lowered his head, resting his forehead against the door frame. "Don't you think I tried?"

I waited for him to elaborate, and eventually, he turned and said, "I tried. I really tried to hold you, but you slipped right through my fingers. I couldn't hold you, Willa. I don't think anyone could, especially not the person you resented the most."

His words shocked me. I didn't resent him, at least not before Estelle. "What are you talking about?"

"Willa, when was the last time we made love. Not had sex, but actually made love?"

"Men don't care about those things."

"Bullshit. We do care. When is the last time you wanted

me? When was the last time you kissed me because you wanted to, not because you were trying to get pregnant?"

I gaped at him.

"You were so concerned with making a baby, that you forgot I was even there. We were living separate lives. We didn't talk. We didn't laugh together or eat together. How was I supposed to hold you when you were unreachable? I knew you weren't okay. You haven't been for years."

"So, you gave up? You just turned around and found someone else without even trying to talk to me?"

"I did try!" he huffed.

"When did you try? What did you do?"

"I would sit next to you when you were reading."

I remembered that. I was annoyed because it felt like he was hovering. "You never said anything?" I complained.

"Because you never even looked up."

"Because you didn't ever say anything. Just like you didn't look at me when I would sit next to you while you watched football."

"You never made time for me," he said.

"So, you go fuck someone else who will give you the time of day?"

"Yeah!"

I slapped him again. "Fuck you!"

He grabbed my wrist as I lifted my hand to swing again. "Willa, why are you upset with me?"

He angled his body away from me as if sensing I was going to knee him in the balls.

He continued, "Do you even miss me. Not the idea of me. But me?" He shook his head, not giving me room to speak. "No. I don't think you do. I think you might miss the comfortable routine, but I think the reason you're upset is that you're afraid without me, you may never have children. You blame me for your unhappiness, but I'm not the reason you're so unhappy." There was a lull of silence between us. "Would you have been this upset if I had sent you a wedding invitation?"

No. But I wouldn't say that aloud.

"You don't want me," He continued, "You only want the part of me that can give you what you really want—a family. You don't love me, and I know I failed you, Willa, but you made it so hard to love you. You pushed me away every chance you could. You had more of a relationship with that damn dog than you had with me."

Maybe he was right. Perhaps he couldn't hold me. In all honesty, I couldn't even hold myself, but he still hurt me. "Speaking of the dog," I started. "When Bella was a puppy, she woke me in the middle of the night to take her out and there you were, sitting on the back patio in the dark talking to Estelle. You were talking about me, Evan. You were telling her private things—things you never even spoke to me about."

He paled a little, having the decency to look guilty.

I went on. "I know I was difficult to love. My heart had shattered into a million pieces, and I didn't even know how to love myself. You just reinforced the idea that I was unlovable when you told Estelle that I was too selfish to care how you were feeling."

He shook his head. "Why didn't you ever say anything?"

"What was I supposed to say? You were supposed to be the one going through the pain with me, but you weren't sad with me, you were angry that I wasn't there for you. I wanted you to get angry with me, not at me. I wanted you to be on my side."

There was an uncomfortable silence between us, and I finished saying what I had to say. "After I heard you on the phone, I tried to come onto you. To seduce you. To win you back. To show you, I wasn't selfish. But you pushed me away every single time for the next two weeks. After that I stopped trying because to you, I was not only unlovable, I was undesirable."

He rubbed a hand down his face. "It wasn't you. It's—I didn't know how to face you like that."

"Like what?"

"You made me hate myself, Willa. I couldn't have sex with you because I was afraid you would get your hopes up for a baby. I didn't want to watch you go through the pain again."

"You're saying you didn't have sex with me because you were protecting me."

"Yes."

"And seeing you with Estelle was what? You, shielding me from harm?"

He let the jab roll off him. "Estelle reminded me of what we used to have."

"So instead of fixing what was wrong, you thought you'd just get the newer version?" I asked, breathless, "And you call me selfish?"

"I'm not saying what I did was right, but it takes two people to fuck up a marriage, Willa, and I really did try."

"Please, you couldn't get away fast enough! I saw the look on your face when I walked in on you. You were relieved."

He nodded. "I was. It had to end, and I didn't know how to leave you. Neither of us was happy. You knew I was cheating, but you never said anything. Not until you had to face it, and even then, you didn't yell. You didn't react as a normal spouse would, and that's because you had already checked out of our marriage. If you need to hate me, that's okay. Hate me. I don't know if we could've repaired our relationship, but we stopped working together a long time ago."

It was over.

I leaned against the railing of the porch, feeling a sense of calm. "So that's it, huh? Your grandma would be disappointed in us."

"I think a lot of people were disappointed, but they don't know the intimate details behind the scenes."

I sighed, feeling exhausted. I didn't want to hate him. Hating him took too much energy, and I was so drained.

"Our house went into contract yesterday," I told him. "I'm going over in the next week to move things out. Is there anything you want? I found some of your keepsakes in the attic."

"And you didn't burn them?" he asked, half-joking.

"I was too tired to put that much effort into burning things. I'm putting the furniture in a storage unit until I figure out a more permanent living situation, but I can't see needing to furnish a whole house so if there is anything you want, please take it."

"Would it be too strange if I helped you move?" he asked.

I nodded. "I'm still really angry at you, so I don't know if that's a good idea. Plus, my dad will be there, and he doesn't have the highest opinion of you anymore."

He shrugged and said, "There are a few things I want to pick up, but I don't have a key."

"Okay, I'll let you know when I'm there this week." I turned and walked down the steps.

"Willa," he called.

I turned back to him.

"I'm glad you didn't hold back. I think this is the first real conversation we've had in years."

I stared at him while I took that in, then confessed, "I broke our plates."

His mouth gaped. "The custom homemade stoneware we picked out?" He sounded so shocked, and I felt vindicated.

"I always thought it was too much to spend on plates," I confessed.

"They were one of a kind," he said, getting angry. "How did they break?"

"I was going to sell them but thought it was more thera-peutic to smash them against concrete. But, hey, at least I didn't burn your stuff."

He was gawking at me, and God did it feel good to tell the truth.

I went into marriage thinking death was the only thing that could separate us, and though there were many times I felt I was dying, Evan and I were both still here. I used to be naïve, thinking everyone met their prince charming. I'd learned about love from watching my parents and Disney movies which were equally sweet and sappy. But later, I found out that my parent's relationship was exceptional, and Disney sugar-coated the Hell out of Grimm's folklore, turning them into happy tales for children.

I didn't need a prince to live my happily whatever may come. I just needed to love myself, and I was learning how.

I smiled to myself, saying, "I'll see you in a few days."

When I walked away, it was with confidence and not the kind driven by anger which is what led me here, but a confidence borne from a place of acceptance.

I was in my bedroom removing my tux jacket when I heard someone enter the room. I turned, expecting Addison, but Travis was coming toward me. He socked me under my left eye, and I stumbled back, completely taken off guard.

"What the fuck!" I shouted as he shoved me.

"Are you out of your Goddamn mind, Oliver?"

My cheek was bleeding, and I belatedly realized he was yelling at me over Addison and me splitting up, but I didn't owe him an explanation. He propelled me toward this decision when he slept with her, and she must have gone straight to him for comfort after we talked because we had only been home for an hour, and we spent half of that time talking.

I stood upright and stalked toward Travis, throwing my own punches. At that moment, we were no longer buddies. We no longer had to pose in wedding photos. We were rivals beating the shit out of one another.

Addison came in, screaming at us to stop, but we didn't, not until we were both in too much pain to continue. We were sprawled out on the floor by the time it was over, both of us with bleeding faces and bruised fists.

Addison stood in the doorway with her arms crossed. "Did you guys get it out of your system?" She asked, not the least bit impressed or amused.

Then she turned into Doctor Addison Arthur MD, checking our wounds and telling us how stupid we were.

I cut her off in the middle of her lecturing me. "When did you know you loved him?"

"What?" she asked, surprised.

I turned to Travis, who was sitting on the floor with his back propped against the bed. I asked him, "How long have you been in love with her?"

He looked exhausted. "I'm so tired of this bullshit," he said on a sigh. "Oliver, you want to know the truth?"

"That's what I'm asking for."

"Since we were seventeen, and I had to walk the new girl to her first class where my best friend in the entire world, the one person I could always count on, asked her out. I tried for years to stop thinking about her, but she was always there. We were twenty before we realized we both had feelings for one another. Things spiraled from there."

I looked at Addison to confirm Travis was telling the truth and she closed her eyes and nodded.

"So, for the past eight years, you two have been—"

"No," Addison said, "We haven't been together since before our engagement."

Travis supplied, "When you told me you were going to propose, I knew it had to stop, and the only way for that to work was if we didn't see each other."

"That's why you took that job in Phoenix?" I asked.

He nodded.

I turned to Addison. "If you loved him, why didn't you break up with me?"

"Because I loved you too. We had a life together, Oli. I was really happy with you, but Travis had me all tied up when he was around. What I felt for Travis was separate from my feelings for you. I loved you both."

"We've been engaged for almost two years, so that still means it was going on for six years."

"It's not like we were fucking like rabbits," Travis interjected, "It only happened when we couldn't keep it from happening."

"What does that mean? Oops, I tripped, and my penis slipped into your vagina again. I guess we just keep rubbing together until it's all better."

"You're the one who asked for the truth," Travis said.

"I'm still asking. What do you mean you couldn't keep it from happening?"

"Come on," Travis said. "Haven't you had a moment where it was physically painful not to touch someone. And it doesn't matter how close you get because it will never be enough, and you just lose control."

I had felt that way, but only recently and it wasn't with Addison.

I must have made a face, because Travis said, "See, you have."

"It was the woman from the hotel," Addison said.

I didn't want to hurt her, but we needed to clear the air even if it was excruciating. "Her name is Willa. She doesn't trust many people, and in an effort to become friends, we promised we would only tell each other the truth, even if it was ugly, even if it made us look bad."

"Are you asking if I want the ugly truth?" Addison asked.

"Yes."

"Yes, Oli, I want the ugly truth."

"I think I would've been content to stay married to you if I hadn't met Willa, but she woke this part of me I didn't even know existed. I didn't know anything was missing until I felt them with her. I realized I need someone who will argue with me.

"I love you, Addison, but I got so wrapped up in fitting myself into your plan for the future, that I forgot how to live my own life. I wish I could go back in time a change that. I obviously haven't been tuned into what's happening around me, or I think I would've at least had some suspicion of you two."

"Are you going to go after her?" Addison asked me.

"I think I'd have a better chance at regaining her trust once you and I are no longer married. But even then, I don't know where she lives. I don't even have her last name. I know her ex-husband's full name."

They were both giving me strange looks, and Travis said, "I thought you guys were totally honest with each other."

"We were, but we shared meaningful things, not our profile information. Actually, that's not true. She has all of my information, but I don't see her reaching out anytime soon."

30

Boxes were packed and lined against the entry wall. My dad and his friend were loading the moving van while I stood in the dining room looking at the last of the furniture.

The last week of packing and moving had been emotionally exhausting. Evan and I went through our things which was tough because a good portion of the items were neither his nor mine. They belonged to Mr. and Mrs. Durban, but that couple no longer existed. Separating our things was like opening old memories only to watch them burn to ash, all the while pretending it didn't feel like a cheese grater to the heart. I didn't want to be reminded of happy times with Evan, because it made me remember our love.

Separating Mrs. Durban from Willa felt almost like I was tearing my left side from my right and letting all the messy insides spill out all over the floor. That's what the last week had been. But I had made it through. I was Willa again, and I was scooping up my blood and guts to sew myself back together.

I was so happy that Jodi's friendship wasn't contingent on my last name. I didn't know how I would have gone through this last year without her or my parents. I didn't need Evan or Oliver.

Shit.

"What's that look?" Jodi asked as she entered the room.

"This has been a long few weeks."

"You're almost done. Everything will feel better when you no longer have to deal with Evan. All that's left is the furniture you're selling. One more week and you'll be able to relax into your new life, and you still have almost two more months of summer break. Maybe we can go away for a weekend sometime. I'll start working on my husband now."

"That sounds amazing! Do you think James will be okay staying home with the kids?"

"Well he's gonna have to be okay with it."

I smiled. I needed something to look forward to, and a girl's getaway was just the kind of thing I needed.

Evan and I had sorted the furniture we wanted and the leftovers we moved into the dining room, so I could take pictures and post them for sale online.

Jodi had the whole day off from her kids so she could help me move. I found a cute little cape cod house in town that a retired couple was renting out. It was perfect with a big backyard for Bella to run. It was close to the school where I taught, and it was only a ten-minute drive to my parent's house. But the best part was Jodi lived only a block away.

The house had two bedrooms, but one was relatively small, so I planned to use it as an office. The master bedroom was the entire upstairs, and I loved the idea that it was all mine. I planned to make it as feminine as possible, with fake fur, sparkles and so much pink that even I would second guess my choice. Okay, so maybe I wouldn't take it that far, but it felt good to have a place that was all mine. My new house was going to help me heal and figure out what came next.

Jodi wrapped her arm around my shoulder, saying, "You know I'm going to be at your house all the time. I'll put the kids in bed, and James can deal with them while I come over and have a bottle of wine.

"You think we'll go through a whole bottle?" I asked because opposed to the way I'd behaved my week at the hotel, I wasn't much of a drinker.

"Oh honey, that bottle is just for me. You're gonna have to get your own."

I laughed. "Whatever! Motherhood has made you a lightweight."

She kissed my cheek and stepped toward the cluster of furniture. "So, what are we photographing first?"

"I guess we should start with the table."

I pulled up the camera on my phone and started taking pictures of each of the twelve items.

As she pulled items out for me, she said, "The sooner we get you in your new house, the sooner we can open up the champagne, and you can tell me about your conversation with Evan."

"I don't want my first conversation in my new home to be about Evan," I said.

"You make a good point. You should just tell me now."

"I don't really know what to say. I yelled. We talked. I slapped him twice. He told me I was impossible to love—"

She gasped, "He said what!"

"Relax, it wasn't quite that harsh, or maybe it was. I don't remember our exact words, but it was long overdue. I told him I broke the plates we bought together."

"The ugly ones you spent a fortune on?"

"Yeah."

"You broke them?"

"Into tiny shards. It felt amazing."

"You know you could've made a small fortune, but I bet there is nothing better than burning your ex-husband's money to make you feel better."

"I didn't plan on doing it. It just seemed like the right thing at the time."

"Did Oliver tell you to break them?" she asked. She knew I didn't want to talk about Oliver. I hadn't given her any more information about him, but she knew he got married, so I'm sure she was dying for the details.

"Nice investigative skills, Jodi."

"Is that a *no comment?*"

"It wasn't Oliver's idea. It was mine, but he helped me break them. And I promise you, I will tell you about him, I just really don't want to think about it right now."

"Okay, maybe that will be our talk over champagne."

"No, I don't want to sit around and complain. I want to have happy talks about good things that are happening in our lives."

"Okay, well hurry and take the last two pictures so we can go. It looks like the guys got all the boxes," Jodi said, looking toward the front door where my dad and his friend were carrying the last two boxes out to the truck.

I snapped the last two pictures, and we left.

♥ ♥ ♥

THE FURNITURE WAS MOSTLY IN PLACE, BUT BOXES were scattered everywhere. It was eight o'clock, and Jodi and I had given up for the night.

She popped the champagne and we toasted, "To fresh starts and awesome neighbors."

"Cheers!" I said as we tapped our glasses.

As I took a sip, I looked around my new living room. It was half the size of my last living room, but I loved it. There was no dining room, only a little breakfast nook, and I loved that too. It didn't feel small. It felt just right. Even with naked walls and boxes everywhere, it felt cozy here. It felt homey, especially with my mom's homemade cupcakes sitting on the kitchen counter.

I grabbed my laptop, tucking it under my arm so I could carry my champagne in one hand and have a hand free to grab a cupcake. I almost tripped over the dog on my way into the living room. She got up and followed me, watching for me to drop crumbs. I sat down on the couch, and she jumped up next to me, her face inches from the cupcake.

"Bella, get down."

Jodi joined me on the couch with her own cupcake. She set her glass on the coffee table and tucked her legs under her before stealing my computer, offering, "I'll post the furniture. You enjoy your champagne and cupcake.

"I won't argue with you doing the work. I'm debating just dropping them at the thrift store, so it's done."

I set my glass down and took a bite of my cupcake while

Jodi opened my computer. As soon as I took my second bite, Jodi gasped.

I realized my mistake instantly.

"What are these?" she asked, before saying, "Oh my God, what is he wearing!"

I tried to grab my computer back from her, but she pulled it away and jumped up, moving across the room as she scrolled through my photos. Every photo I had on my phone was shared with my computer, and she just discovered all the images of Oliver and me.

I sat back down and grabbed my drink because fuck it. I decided at that moment that I wanted to get drunk. As I drank, I watched her face over the glowing screen. I saw her shoulders drop, and her expression change from excitement to worry.

She looked up at me with wide eyes and a worried expression. I swallowed my emotions and shook my head

She spun the computer around, showing me a pic of me, asleep and drooling on Oliver's jacket.

"He took a picture of you sleeping?"

I nodded.

"Did you know he took this?"

"I didn't know about half of those until after I left the hotel. I almost deleted them all, but I couldn't."

"Who was taking the pictures of you together?"

"Some woman we met at the winery."

"You're fucking hot, girl! But what are you wearing? And what's with his romper?"

"We picked outfits for each other."

"That explains a lot, but it doesn't explain why you didn't tell me it was serious."

"It wasn't." I shook my head, barely believing my own words. "We hardly knew each other. It was nothing."

"You slept together?"

My silence was an admission.

She blew up a photo and turned it toward me. It crushed me, and she must have seen me flinch because she said, "Okay, so you not only slept together, you fell for him, and he obviously felt something for you, or he wouldn't have snapped a picture of you sleeping. And you can see the chemistry through these damn photos. The way he's looking at you . . . "

I pulled my knees up to my chest, feeling foolish. "I thought so, but he married her. It's . . . I mean, you should've seen them together. You think you see chemistry, but it was nothing in comparison to the way he looked at Addison."

"I don't believe it," she said, continuing to scroll back through.

"I was his rebound," I said, "I don't think he meant for it to happen, but when he saw her again all those feeling must have come back because . . . because I believed he loved me back. There was this crazy connection between us, like his broken heart called to mine. I knew it was a bad idea. I did, and I tried to be smart, but Jodi—"

"But you fell in love with him."

"I swear it's not as crazy as it sounds."

"I want you to tell me everything," she said, sitting next to me and twisting to face me.

I nodded.

"I mean every single detail," she reiterated.

"Okay," I agreed and then began, "When I arrived at the

hotel, Oliver was there at the front desk with a bottle of Pink Moscato."

I WAS ON MY FIFTH GLASS OF CHAMPAGNE BY THE TIME I finished my story. "I saw the photos of them dancing together on their wedding day. So, there is nothing left to do, but get over him," I said, wiping my eyes and shrugging. "I deserve better than that. I just wish he was the guy I thought he was."

Jodi pulled another tissue out of the box, wiping her tears and blowing her nose before adding it to the tower she'd been building. "There had to be something that made him go back to Addison. Like, maybe someone was being held hostage and would only be released if Oliver went through with the wedding or something."

God, I loved my best friend. Only she would come up with something so outrageous. "Or he just loved her," I said.

"Well then, we will find someone better," She said, picking up my computer. She began typing away.

"What are you doing?" I was afraid to ask.

"I'm signing you up for online dating. And then I'm going to track Oliver down and murder him for hurting you. And you can't object. You wouldn't let me kill Evan, so you have to let me get this one."

"I can't handle life without you, Jodi. I won't let you go to jail on my behalf."

"Fine, then the least you can do is let me find someone for you. Online dating works. I know so many couples that met that way."

"I don't know the first thing about dating, and I'm not sure I'm ready for that."

"Well, while you're getting yourself ready to date, you can go on practice dates."

I shook my head. I would fight her later.

31

WILLA

*I*t'd been two months since the house sold and school was getting ready to start. My new house felt like a real home. I didn't go overkill on the pink, but the bedroom was incredibly feminine.

I had a good tan from the week before when Jodi and I took our girls trip. I rarely let my skin get very dark. It stemmed from my childhood when I'd been self-conscious because I didn't want to look different from my parents. With a tan, my skin was the color of creamy milk chocolate. It was liberating and made me feel beautiful.

I got to tell Jodi all about the disasters of online dating. I received so many dick pics and terrible pickup lines. Then there were the super direct men who were not interested if you didn't put out on the first date. They weren't all assholes. Some of them were just weird or awkward.

I had Jodi laughing so hard she had tears streaming down her face. She was still determined to find me, Mr. Right. I told her to get me a vibrator, and I'd name it Mr. Right, but she didn't think that was funny.

Oliver called me three weeks ago. I'd answered, but when I realized it was him, I hung up. Addison had announced her pregnancy on social media, not that I was looking or anything. I wanted to be happy for him, but I wasn't. I was angry and hurt. He reaffirmed my belief that men could not be trusted.

He left me a voicemail explaining he got my number from when he called his dad from my phone. He asked me to give him a chance to explain things. I sent him a text asking him to please never contact me again.

I didn't receive any more calls, but he texted me good morning every day for two weeks before I blocked his number. I hated him. His wife was pregnant, and he was seeking me out. What the fuck?

I looked at myself in the mirror as I applied lipstick. I was never a lipstick person before, but it made me feel pretty, and this was the summer for reinvention, so I decided I was now a lipstick person. I put the lid back on the tube and spun to Bella, who was lying in the bathroom door watching me. "How do I look?"

Her ears perked, and she tilted her head to the side. I laughed and said, "Do you want to go outside?"

She flopped her head the other way, and when I took a step, she jumped up and ran toward the back door. I let her out and adjusted the thin straps on my new yellow maxi dress. While I was reinventing myself, I discovered I really loved dresses. They were comfy and made me feel pretty. I twisted my hair into a thick braid that wrapped around my shoulder.

I let Bella back in before leaving. I drove to the coffee shop where I had agreed to meet my newest suitor. Jodi found this one. I was pretty sure his profile picture was fake. It looked like a male model's headshot, but I guess I would find out soon enough.

The August evening was hot, and the sun was bright as I pulled into the parking lot. I walked inside and didn't see my date, so I got a drink and sat at a table facing the door.

While I watched the front door, someone came from behind me. My whole body froze as Oliver sat across from me in his ridiculous pineapple romper and short hair. "Hey, duckling."

I scooted back in my chair and stood, ready to leave.

He sat up straighter and said, "Addison and I are no longer married. We broke up during our reception. If I had never met you, I might have been happy with Addison, but she dulled in compassion to you.

"Willa, you brought me to life. She came to the hotel that morning to tell me she was pregnant and begged me to give her a chance and I thought I could try, but it's not fair to anyone. I couldn't leave her at the alter because I couldn't embarrass her like that. I care about Addison. Part of me will always care about her because she's been a huge part of my life and she's going to have my baby. But I'm in love with you, Willa, and I'm so sorry I hurt you."

I shook my head. "Not this time, Oliver. I politely asked for you to stop contacting me, which you ignored. I had your number blocked which should've been a sign I wasn't playing hard to get. I don't know how you found me here, but I'm not interested." With my cup in hand, I walked out of the coffee shop without looking back.

"Willa," I heard behind me.

I kept walking, determined not to let him hurt me. Not

this time, except seeing him did hurt. It fucking hurt because it reminded me how real it felt. It made me remember how I had let him in only for him to destroy me, or at least he would have if I weren't so well acquainted with agony.

Oliver followed me out, saying, "I know you're angry, but you felt it too. You know what we have is real, and it's worth fighting for."

I spun on him. I pursed my lips, trying to stop myself from speaking, but the words came anyway. "Let me get this right, you broke up with your pregnant wife at your wedding reception, and I'm supposed to feel okay about this because you're in love with me?"

"Addison isn't in love with me either. She loves me, but we aren't a match. She's a rose, delicate, high maintenance, and beautiful. Her thorns stuck in me years ago, and I just thought that was it, but then I met you, and you're a fucking wildflower, spontaneous, tough, and gorgeous."

"Ha," I laughed. "See that's the thing, Oliver, I might look like Queen Anne's lace, but I'm Hemlock. I might look harmless, but I will fuck you up if you don't leave me alone." I turned toward the parking lot.

"I don't know what those are, but I know you love me too."

I spun back to him. "What gives you the impression that I want anything to do with you?"

He rocked from heel to toe in his stupid highlighter shoes. "Because you got my tattoo."

"What?" I asked.

"Unless I'm wrong and that isn't an olive branch on your left shoulder."

My breath came heavily, and my heart raced. "It's an

olive branch right in the spot you requested," I admitted, "but it's not for you. It's for me, to remind me that what we had was real and special and so easily broken. You made me fall for you, but love isn't enough, Oliver. Not for me. Not anymore."

Oliver said, "You're wrong, Willa. You're afraid. What I did to you was awful, but I'm not going anywhere this time. All I'm asking for is a chance. You saw me at my worst. I was confused before, but I know what I want, Willa. I want you."

I rolled my eyes. "Oliver, I saw you and Addison together in the hotel. The love between you is stronger than anything you've shown me. She will always be a part of your life. She should be. You're having a kid together, but I won't share you with Addison. I need someone whose love doesn't feel like a competition. I will always worry about you leaving me for your ex. You don't want that, and before you try to explain yourself further, I understand the situation. If I were you, I probably would've married her too, but it made me unable to trust you, Oliver, and I won't start a relationship with someone I don't trust."

"What can I do?" he asked.

"Stop trying to reach out. I won't change my mind."

I watched as it sunk in. I did love him, and I hated him for making me walk away again, but a relationship with trust issues would be a bad relationship, and I wouldn't set myself up for failure.

Oliver didn't try to stop me as I left, and as soon as I got back onto the road, I cried for what could have been.

♥ ♥ ♥

Bella was snuggling next to me on the couch when Jodi let herself in the front door, saying, "I love you so much girl, but what is wrong with you?"

I paused the show I was watching and looked to Jodi who readjusted her youngest daughter on her hip. She was in a tizzy about something, and I wasn't in the mood. I was still raw from leaving Oliver an hour ago.

While Bella went to greet our new guests, I said, "Listen, Jodi, whatever this is, can it wait? I've had a really rough evening."

"Well, I'm about to make it much easier," she said, but the way she said it gave me the impression things were only going to get worse.

Jodi asked, "What did you to say to Oliver to make him back off?"

I tilted my head in question because how did she know about Oliver. And then I put it together. She was the one that set me up with the fake profile picture guy.

"You set me up?" I asked in disbelieving anger.

"You bet your ass I did. Six weeks ago, I wrote Oliver a nasty private message scolding him for hurting my best friend. He wrote back, telling me how he had messed up. He begged me to give him your number and put in a good word for him. I refused. He begged for your last name, and I refused, but he wrote to me every single day. He told me the annulment would take too long, so they did a dissolution. He sent me documents as proof. And the whole time, I was sending him the photos of the guys you were going on dates with because he hurt you so he should feel hurt or jealous."

Her daughter started fussing, and she rearranged her and started swaying as she continued talking, "I thought you were moving on, but then you got that tattoo and gave me some bullshit about it being a reminder that anything can fall apart when really, it's because you don't want to get over him. You're both crazy about one other, so I thought I'd get you two together and let you guys figure it out, but then I get a call from him, saying he's backing off. So, what did you say to him?"

"Jodi . . . " I was almost speechless. "You're the last person I would expect to side with Oliver."

"I'm not siding with Oliver. I'm siding with love." Her baby started crying, so she came over and sat on the coffee table across from me, bouncing her curly-headed one-year-old daughter. As she bounced the babe, she looked at me, saying, "Sweetie, I think you're making a mistake. I've tried so hard not to say anything, but he's crazy about you. Every day, for the last six weeks, Oliver has sent me something he loves about you." She slipped her phone out of her pocket and pulled up her messages, handing it to me.

August 9th: The smell of her hair.

August 8th: Ice cream smudges across her face.

August 7th: Her blissful smile after she's had a bite of chocolate ice cream.

August 6th: Her Spice Girls' dance routine.

August 5th: Her ability to get completely submerged in a book.

August 4th: Her strength.

August 3rd: The flush in her cheeks when she finally gives in to her desires.

August 2nd: Wanting the truth even when it's ugly.

August 1st: Her ability to laugh at herself.

July 31st: The way her hair flows out behind her when she runs.

July 29th: The way she feels tucked into my side sleeping.

July 28th: Naming her dog Birdie.

July 27th: When she dared me to do the Macarena, but then joined me so I wouldn't have to do it alone.

July 26th: Her ability to come up with a reason for a children's spelunking foundation.

July 25th: Her complete lack of knowledge of wine.

July 24th: The way she pushes her hair back before she takes a drink.

July 23rd: Her dresses.

July 22nd: Her smile when she didn't realize I was watching.

July 21st: Her ability to lose herself in a thought.

July 20th: Her fearlessness.

July 19th: The way her mind works.

July 18th: Her ability to laugh in the midst of pain.

I scrolled down.

June 27th: I love the way she folds hamburger wrappers.

June 26th: I love that she thinks ice cream can be a meal if she wants it to be.

June 25th: I love that she calls me Oliver when I told her everyone calls me Oli.

June 24th: I love those jean shorts.

June 23rd: I love that she opened up to me.

June 22nd: I loved that she offered me a corkscrew even when she wasn't sure about me.

June 21st: I love her expressive dark eyes.

June 20th: I love her beautiful skin that gives her an air of mystery.

When I looked up, Jodi was standing rocking from side to side, her baby half-asleep in her arms. I was trying desperately not to cry.

Jodi whispered, "He said Addison knows he's in love with you."

"He lives in New York, Jodi. Even if we tried, it wouldn't work. I'm not moving there, and he can't come here. Not with a child in the picture."

Jodi said, "But will you regret it if you don't try?"

I couldn't answer her. I didn't know which was worse, risking it, or wondering what could have been.

She continued, "He's staying at the Edgemont Hotel, room 216."

32

I held my breath as I knocked at the door. It was early. Too early to be knocking at someone's door. I hadn't gone to the hotel the night before because I kept finding reasons not to, but I didn't sleep. Not a wink. I came early because I was afraid I'd miss him.

I waited with bated breath, impatient for the door to open, but terrified of the man behind the door.

Then it was opening, and I was gathering the words I had prepared. My mouth was open, ready to speak when I saw her blonde hair and blue eyes. Addison was answering Oliver's hotel room door, and I had never wanted super-speed as much as I did at that moment. I let out a breath, and with no idea what to say to her, I began walking away.

"Willa?" she called, stepping out into the hall.

I turned to her. She was fully dressed and looked beautiful, like a fucking rose. Oliver got that part right. She was pristine, a mascot for femininity. But something I hadn't been able to tell from photos was how intimidating she was, not only for her beauty but for the sharp intelligence behind those baby blue eyes.

I would never measure up to her, and I think she knew it. She didn't know what Oliver saw in me and staring at Miss Perfection, I didn't know what he saw in me either.

She said, "He told me you turned him down."

I nodded. "I did."

"But you're having second thoughts?" she questioned.

"Not anymore," I said, and before I could leave, she closed the hotel door and stepped toward me.

"Let's get a drink in the lobby," she said in a tone that made it difficult to decline.

"Oh-kay." We walked to the elevator in silence.

As we rode down to the lobby, she said, "Oliver went for a run this morning. He runs more when he's upset. You've turned him into a pretzel. He's all twisted up and doesn't know what to do with himself."

This was by far the strangest conversation I had ever been a part of, and I wasn't even an active member.

The doors opened, and we walked out into the lobby, making a left into the lounge. I got a coffee while Addison fixed a green tea for herself, and we sat at a table by the windows overlooking the front of the hotel.

"I know this is probably strange for you," she said with a laugh, "It's strange for me too, but I'd like us to be friends because the truth is, I'm not going anywhere, Willa. I will always be a part of Oli's life. I'm having his child." She placed a hand on her belly that was just beginning to show a slight bump.

She continued, "He has sacrificed so much for me. He's

followed along with my life plan and made every transition so much easier for me. He took care of me in med school. When I was gone for long hours, he'd pack me a lunch, or fill my car with gas, or bring me meals. He would do all the random things I was too exhausted to do and never complained. That's who he is. That's what he's always done for me. If he loved me enough to do those things for me, I can only imagine what he will do for our daughter."

"It's a girl?" I asked.

"Yeah, we found out the other day," she said with a sweet smile, obviously adoring the bump growing in her belly. Then with a serious look, she said, "Oliver came here to see you. I came here to interview for jobs. Cincinnati is just over the river, and there are a lot of options for me."

I was afraid to get my hopes up, but it sounded like she was saying—

"Oliver has made every move for me," she said. "It's time I made one for him. He wants to be closer to you. He's been scoping real estate while I've been interviewing."

I shook my head. "I don't understand."

She leaned forward on the table. "I knew he was in love with you before we said our vows. He went through with the wedding because he didn't want to hurt me. I love Oliver, but in all honesty, after we got engaged, things were never the same. Travis moved away, and I began to wonder how much of my staying with Oliver was because I felt guilty and trapped. It's like one morning I woke up and realized I was the villain of my own story, but by then I had a little life growing inside of me. Maybe that's where my sudden conscience came from because that little voice is the reason I told Oliver about Travis and me. It's the reason he left and found you.

"You opened his eyes to all the twisted things I'd put him through, and in the meantime, all I could think about was how I didn't know how to do life without him. He was the one holding me together. Travis was there for me, but he doesn't treat me the way Oliver does, or at least the way Oliver used to treat me.

"I was unfair to him in so many ways, but when I saw how much it hurt him to leave you, I knew his love for me had changed."

I sat up straighter, asking, "Are you still in love with him?"

"I was only in love with how much he loved me. I know how bad that makes me sound, but that's my honest truth. I didn't realize what I was doing to him until I saw the tears he cried for you during our wedding. That's when I knew I had to let him go."

"And what happens when you change your mind and realize you want him back? You have a child together. You have a history. I can't compete with those things."

"There is no competition. He wants you, and I won't change my mind. Oli and I have run our course."

I swallowed, fingering the cooling cup of coffee. "He's going to be an amazing father," I said, and she nodded.

"Why were you in his room this morning?" I had to ask.

"I had a feeling you would come, and I wanted to meet you. I'm glad you came when you did."

"You really think we can be friends?" I asked.

"I don't know, but I'd like to be."

I nodded. "Do you know when he'll be back?"

"It might be awhile. He left just before you came."

"Will you tell him to call me?" I asked, pulling out my phone to unblock his number.

"Of course," she said with a smile.

33

OLIVER

I peeked in the window of the front door like a peeping tom. Willa was asleep on the couch with her dog lying between her legs. The dog perked up, looking at me with her head twisting to the side. I didn't want to wake her, so I moved back and sat on the stoop outside. It was a quaint neighborhood with mature trees lining the sidewalks. Each house differed from the next, but all appeared equally loved. I felt like this was a neighborhood where everyone waved to one another. It wasn't exactly a small town, but it had a small-town feel.

As I waited, a few people walked by, and I was right, everyone waved to one another.

"What are you doing over here?" I heard and looked up to see Jodi walking toward me with a double stroller and a five-year-old boy dragging along behind.

I said, "Willa came by the hotel this morning. I wasn't there, but I guess she and Addison talked. Addie said she wanted me to call her."

Jodi laughed, "So obviously you come over with a bottle of Pink Moscato and a bouquet of . . . weeds?"

"They're wildflowers," I corrected.

"They're ugly," she said.

"It's supposed to be a gesture."

"Of what?"

"It's . . . " I paused, looking at the bouquet of half-dead weeds. "Okay, I'll do it without them," I said, putting them down.

"Come here," she said, turning the stroller around and calling out to the little boy who was wandering around Willa's yard. He turned and ran back toward his mom.

She walked me two houses down and pointed at the flowerbed. "Pick some of those and take them to her. It's a prettier gesture."

"I'm not going to pick flowers out of someone's yard."

"Sure you are. This is my house, and there are roses over there," she said, pointing.

"Roses are overrated. Is there anything else?"

We took a stone path along the side of the house into Jodi's backyard. There were a variety of flowers, but none were quite right. Then I noticed the empty lot behind her house. "Who owns that lot?"

"I don't know. The city is the one who comes out to mow it. Why?"

Without answering, I walked back and crossed the little alley into the open lot. Along the edges were knee-high weeds, and among them, I found Queen Anne's lace. After Willa had mentioned them, I looked it up, and though its beauty didn't compare to her, I thought it'd make a strong point. I picked a bushel and carried them back into Jodi's yard.

When I reached her, I said, "Did you know Queen Anne's lace is actually wild carrot?"

She was giving me a strange look, and eyed the wild-flowers in my hand, saying, "So what you're saying is you're going to give her a bouquet of carrot stems instead of roses?"

I nodded with a smile, "Yeah, and I think she'll love it." I looked at them. The cluster of soft white flowers looked delicate, but they were hardy and a pain in the ass to pick.

Jodi offered, "Let me grab some scissors so you can at least cut the ends to make it look less . . . umm, less like you picked them out of a field."

It was obvious she doubted me, and I knew how well she knew Willa, so it had me second-guessing myself.

34

I was pouring myself a cup of coffee and fretting over why Oliver hadn't called when there was a knock at the front door. Bella barked, and then stood at the door wagging her tail, excited for company.

I saw a shadow through the window but whoever knocked must be standing off to the side. Jodi and my parents were the only ones who visited, but they all had keys and rarely knocked.

I opened the door, and the first thing I noticed was Trey, Jodi's five-year-old son driving his trucks along the cement path up to my front porch. Then I saw Jodi casually standing on the sidewalk with her double stroller. She was watching with a grin, and I gave her a questioning look as Bella went out to greet Trey.

Jodi pointed next to me, and that's when I noticed the man who had knocked. Oliver wore regular clothes this time, and he had a bottle of Pink Moscato in one hand and a bouquet of Queen Anne's lace in the other. I covered my mouth as I stepped toward him. The tears came before I had a chance to hold them back. I took the flowers that he held out and crushed him in a hug.

When we pulled apart, his thumb wiped my tears, and he leaned in to kiss me, but Bella interrupted us by nudging between us. She didn't like it when I shared my affection with other people. She jumped up on me, further separating me from Oliver.

"Bella," I laughed.

When I was a suitable distance away, she turned to say hello to Oliver.

I looked out to Jodi. "Did you do this?" I asked, pointing to Oliver.

She shook her head. "Nope. I just came across him and had to see how this would go down."

I laughed, saying, "We'll talk later." I turned back to Oliver and Bella. He was kneeling and petting her as her body danced, shaken by her wagging tail. I called, "Bella, inside."

Then I grabbed Oliver's free hand and pulled him inside, closing the door between us and our audience. I set my flowers down on the entry table and took his face between my hands and kissed him.

His arms wrapped around me and Bella whined. We ignored her and kept kissing. She let out a long sigh and flopped on the floor.

I pulled back, saying, "Bella has never really had to share my affection before. This will be a transition for her."

"We can take it slow," he said with a smirk. "Because we're good at that."

"You brought me some wine?"

"Your favorite," he said, holding out the bottle of Pink Moscato.

"You know Pink Moscato is not actually my favorite drink, right?" before he could answer, I continued, "but seeing as it's the reason we met, it will always have a special place in my heart."

"Willa, look at it," he said, pointing at the bottle.

I inspected the label which read Pink f*cking Moscato. I burst into laughter. "How did you do that?"

"I found a place that does custom labels, but apparently, they don't believe in cursing."

"I lied. This is my favorite drink."

Oliver smiled, "Mine too. Screw bourbon. I love Pink fucking Moscato."

Willa

We lived gratefully ever after. We weren't always happy, but that's the way life is, and I preferred the ugly truth opposed to the lie of a happily ever after. Oliver and I loved each other, and we worked through the hard days together. Our life together was complicated and imperfect, but Oliver brought me so much joy as did his sweet daughter.

Life could be its own unique torture, and sometimes sadness came in unpredictable waves, but sometimes beauty grew out of ugly circumstances. Heartbreak made us more aware of everything we had to cherish, and I treasured the life we built together.

I held my soon-to-be stepdaughter in my arms and knew that I would love her forever. She just turned a year old, and we were celebrating her birthday. Judging by the number of people who showed up, she might be the most spoiled girl ever born.

Addison came in the back door, balancing a cake in her hands with Bella at her heels. She entered the kitchen bending to kiss baby Emerson on the cheek, saying, "How's my baby?"

"Ma-ma!" Emerson threw her arms up, and Addison set down the cake before taking her daughter in her arms. Addison's job demanded a lot of her time, but she loved what she did. She had a house two streets over, but also had an apartment in the city, so she didn't have to make the drive every day. I took the year off teaching to stay home with Emerson, and I loved that I could be such a huge part of her life.

Oliver came up from behind me, wrapping his arms around me. He kissed my shoulder, and I placed my hand on his arm before spinning to kiss him. We had talked about trying to have a baby, but it terrified me to go through everything again. I knew this time things would be different, but we decided to wait to meet with a fertility specialist until after we got married. It was hard to believe it was only a few weeks away. We planned an intimate ceremony on the beach with only our closest friends and family. I couldn't wait.

Our cozy house was packed. Jodi and her family were there. Oliver's parents, who had finally accepted our dynamic, sat with their spouses in the living room, looking uncomfortable as they listened to Jodi talk about breastfeeding. I stifled a laugh and watched Addison sit down next to her mother. Her father hadn't come, and I knew his absence hurt her, but he was still not speaking to her after everything that had happened.

Travis sat on the other side of Addison, playing with the baby in her arms. He was trying to teach Emerson to fist bump, but her chubby little hands just kept grabbing at his beard. Eventually, Emerson crawled into Travis's lap while Addison talked to her mother. I wondered if Addison would end up with Travis, but so far, they seemed to remain only good friends, but he loved baby Emerson almost as much as Oliver loved her.

In a way, I got the big family I always hoped for. We got some weird looks whenever we explained our situation, but it worked for us. Truth be told, I loved Addison. She and I were complete opposites, and we didn't always agree, but we accepted each other the way we were, and we made our unusual dynamic work because we all loved Emerson.

Like I said, the most spoiled little girl ever born.

I turned in Oliver's arms. "Well, Mr. Moscato, I think this party is a success."

He leaned in, whispering, "All because of you, Willa. You're incredible." His lips brushed mine. "I can't wait for you to become Mrs. Pink Moscato."

AUTHOR NOTE

This story is purely fiction, but I have lived through the sorrow labeled infertility. Several of my friends have also lived through a variation of the same struggle. I never wanted to write my story about infertility because it would be a pretty miserable read, but I want people to know they are not alone.

I left a job because of our infertility struggle. I worried over our marriage, battled anxiety and depression, and went into debt because of our struggle. I distanced myself from friends, family, and even my husband. Our marriage could have fallen apart, and sometimes, I worried it would. For a while, we were in very different places emotionally, and I can't stress this enough, fertility medications made me crazy. I didn't want my husband to see all the emotions I was feeling, so I tried to hide them from him, and instead appeared distant and unloving.

At a very pivotal point in our struggle, through the grace of God, we fell together instead of falling apart. Our insecurities fought to divide us, but we made it through, partly because we were too stubborn and loyal to give up on one another, but also because our love is real. It may not be perfect, but we've committed to loving one another even when it takes the extra effort, and because of this, we have something beautiful. We are enough, even if we never have children.

Since we stopped trying, I have been able to enjoy the kids in my life so much more. They feel like a blessing instead of a heartbreaking reminder of what we may never have.

For those of you who tell struggling couples to, "Just relax, and it will happen." Stop. Please, please, please, I beg of you, stop! I said things like this before I understood the struggle—before I knew how words meant to encourage can break a person's spirit. Most likely, you have no idea what the couple is going through. For medical reasons, we are either trying, or we are actively preventing pregnancy. So, when someone tells me to relax, that person is lucky I don't throat punch them. I know most say it with good intentions. I'm not asking anyone to walk on eggshells, but don't assume you know what is best for someone else. If you need to say something, instead of offering empty encouragement, empathize with them.

Infertility is a unique pain. To the world, I looked whole, but for a while, my grief was all-consuming. The bitterness I felt was unexpected, and it made me hate myself. I didn't want the ugly, indignant thoughts that filled my head. Every baby announcement or baby shower, every time I heard someone complain about their kids, I would feel all these things that made me disgusted with myself. I was so miserable and hateful that I didn't know how to be happy for others. That is an ugly place to be, friends.

It took me a long time to separate what I was going through with what other people had going on. After our failed IVF, I decided for my wellbeing I had to stop. I couldn't keep hating myself and my life. I took down the crib we'd had up for years and turned it into a relaxing room where I do most of my writing. My mind was so consumed with the baby struggle that for years, I barely made time to write.

Once we stopped trying, I buried myself in my writing. It was my therapy. It was a way to immerse myself in something that took my mind off my situation.

People encouraged me to write about our struggle, but writing about infertility was the last thing I wanted to do. Now that I have had some time to heal, I thought I would incorporate it into a story. What makes this story so beautiful to me is its realness, its suffering, its wrong decisions because nobody is perfect, and the brokenhearted realizing their worth.

Even though there are so many going through the same struggle, it can still feel very isolating. To those who are fighting infertility, and trying to get pregnant, you are so brave and so strong. I didn't know my own courage and strength until I fought with all I had for something that meant everything to me. I had forty-seven failed cycles, and each time I picked myself up and kept going with hope for the next time. We went through so many treatments, and I learned to be brave and bold because there was no other option.

One of the hardest things you can do is to keep going in

the midst of your struggle. And for those of you who need a time out or have to call it, you are not a failure. Knowing your limit is essential. You are important and resilient. And most importantly, you are enough. Don't let anyone make you feel like you aren't enough. Learn to love yourself and your life, because as much as we try to plan our lives, we don't know what the future holds.

ACKNOWLEDGMENTS

Thank you to all my readers!

And to everyone who put up with me through my worst moments, thank you!

Mary Catherine Kline, I don't have the words for all you have done for me. You believed in me from the very beginning and encouraged me through every step. You were a light in my world and life feels a lot dimmer without you.

To my mom. My hero. Thanks for always being there for me. Thank you for encouraging me to write this story.

Sarah Ware, you are my Jodi. I think you probably already knew that, but I am so unbelievably blessed to have someone so caring and strong in my life to encourage me. You managed to keep your kind heart through all the tough times. You are a badass, and an inspiration.

Heather Coates, thank you for your vulnerability. Sometimes being brave means exposing the unpleasant things instead of hiding them. You've shown me that it's okay to be vulnerable and bold in asking for help. I'm so grateful to have you in my life.

Melissa Di Rienzo, my dear friend, thank you for being the first to read this story and being with me through the whole process. You are the first person I go to with all of my questions, and I love that you're always excited to help. You rock! I don't know what I'd do without you.

Brenda Perkins, thank you for taking a girl's trip with me to Cincinnati. You didn't know at the time that you were going to say something that would inspire me to write a scene that would turn into a story and then a novel. Thanks for being uniquely you! And thank you for being there for me on one of the worst days of my life.

To Tim Rezes, the best father-in-law a girl could ask for, thank you for cheering for me. I'm always thrilled to hear your feedback and amazed at your attention to detail. Thanks for believing in me, and thank you for teaching your son what it means to be a good man.

Jenna Abrahamson, I think you gave me the best compliment of all, comparing my work to one of my all-time favorite authors. Thank you for all your encouragement.

Thank you, Sara Wilson, and to everyone in our Monday writing group. You have all encouraged me to keep writing, and your critiquing continues to make me a better writer.

Marissa thank you for all your support through the years.

Lisa, thank you for lending your keen eye and catching those difficult to find errors.

Justin, my husband and best friend, thank you for fighting through the trenches with me. Writing this story was emotional. It is so easy to grow apart, and our story could have turned out much differently if we hadn't been so stub-

born in our love for one another. Thank you for all your reas-
surances when I got too wrapped up in this story and forgot
what was real and what was in my head. Thank you for
believing in me. No matter what may come, you are my
gratefully ever after.

Other Books from Anna Rezes

Valla Series:

Coming February 2020

ABOUT THE AUTHOR

ANNA REZES has been passionate about writing since she was a child. When she's not busy honing her superpowers or traveling to other worlds full of fictional characters, she is spending time with family and friends. She lives in Central Ohio with her husband, their two dogs, and the cat they love and hate. Anna is the author of *Unraveling Emily*, *Descendant of Valla*, *Guardian of Latovia*, *Broken Alliance*, and *Pink f*cking Moscato*. For more from Anna Rezes visit:

www.annarezes.com
www.instagram.com/anna_rezes
www.facebook.com/annarezesauthor
www.twitter.com/annarezes